The Deserted Daughters Christmas Wish

Gwyn May

Disclaimer

This story is a work of fiction, any resemblance to people is purely coincidence. All places, names, events, businesses, etc. are used in a fictional manner. All characters are from the imagination of the author.

Table of Contents

Chapter One

April 1875
London

Ten-year old Lizzie Straine woke to an unpleasant odour of unwashed bodies and stale alcohol in the dilapidated room and put her nose under the thin blanket, trying to ignore the musty smell of the grey wool.

Nine other people, adults and children, slept on, in the cramped room, which Lizzie was grateful for as it gave her time to daydream, to slip into an imaginary place in her head where sheep and cattle grazed in lush green fields, surrounded by sprawling hedges and a five-bar gate. Beyond, far-off hills met a cloudless pale blue sky.

She had seen such a scene in a painting hanging in the local pawn-broker's window. The air was clean in her dream place, fresh with a light breeze to glide across her face.

A fog warning sounded out on the estuary, bringing her back to reality.

For a moment she listened intently for the next mournful sound of the bell, alerting sailors to the dangers of rocks invisible in the mist lying on the grey water.

Bill Watson, a dockworker like her father, often spoke of the state of the sea on the morrow. Lizzie learned from last night's conversation the tide would now be at ebb. The water lying almost still, moving gently like a reptilian's skin.

The noise sounded again and young Lizzie thought of the men out there on sailing ships, listening keenly and trying to pin-point the dull chime and steer a clear course out to sea and far-away from the natural hazards close to the shoreline.

Nearby her father coughed several times and then spat phlegm into the spittoon at the side of the make-shift bed he shared with his wife.

Lizzie was aware her mother was beginning to stir and heard her snap at her husband. He spat once more and turned back to his sleep.

Peace reigned for long moments, and Lizzie let go of the breath she was holding and tried to go back to her scene of green tranquillity but it wasn't to be.

People were beginning to stir and the unpleasant noise of early morning escalated, until it was a crescendo of clatter and commotion.

Bill Watson and his two boys climbed out of their beds and into outdoor clothes ready for another day in the dockyard or the back alleys of the slum they called home.

Lizzie waited for her own father to rise, but instead he pulled a blanket to his chin and was snoring in moments.

Her mother gave a long drawn out sigh. Lizzie understood and accepted it would be a day without wages and without supper tonight.

Bill Watson's wife rose and threw a dirty blouse and skirt over the shift she had slept in. In moments she was cuffing her two children and demanding they stack their bed to the side of the room to make floor space for another day in the cramped and airless room.

Edna Watson's voice galvanised Lizzie's mother into action and similarly Sallie Straine began to berate her own three girls. Shouting and swiping anyone that came near her flaying hand. "Get a move on for pity's sake."

Abandoning the scolding of her daughters Sallie Strain went to the window, her youngest child Annie clinging to her neck, and pulled the thin curtain aside and looked out.

A familiar figure came into view and Lizzie's mother quickly dropped the frayed material and turned back into the room.

"Lizzie," she said, hurriedly with an edge of panic to her voice, "I want you to go to the seamstress, at number 42 on Arburton Street. Ask her if there's any sewing she can give us. We won't eat today if there is no work. So put that in your mind when you go begging for a job, however small."

"Can I have a drop of tea and a bit of bread before I go?" Lizzie asked plaintively.

"There's no time. Just get going."

"That's not fair. I hardly had anything to eat last night. Those greedy so-and-so's grabbed most of it," she said pointing at her two younger sisters, five year old Annie and seven year old Martha.

Her father stirred, turning onto his back. "Just do as you're told otherwise I'll get out of this bed and give you a clout you will not forget in a hurry."

Lizzie swallowed, forcing tears back. Her father's words were no idle threat. Her ears would ring for days if he struck her head as he had last time he was in a temper.

Sullen, but without another word, she stepped over the blankets still lying on the floor where they had fallen, and went to the door.

Her eyes raked the chipped paint and dirty handle as she pulled it open and went through, careful to close the door quietly so as not to antagonise her mother further. Otherwise there would be a slap across her back-side that would sting for long minutes after.

Running down the flight of stairs, her bare feet slapping on the wood, Lizzie kept her eyes on the front door. Once she was through that, she would be out on the street in the bitter morning air.

Though there would be no comparison to the image she had in her mind earlier—green fields and contented cattle—at the very least she would be out of striking distance of a belligerent parent and out of the way of Edna Watson too, who took it upon herself to cuff any child in reaching distance, whoever they may belong to.

Once outdoors she ran towards three bigger boys. the tallest leering at her and ready to poke her with the sharp stick he was twirling in his hand. Lizzie sprinted down the cobbled pavement, sticking out her tongue rudely when she judged it safe to do so.

The cobbles beneath the soles of her feet were cold and wet. Keeping her eyes peeled for any sharp stones, broken glass or abandoned objects, she ran on, passing a few small shops selling tired looking vegetables.

The baker's shop door was open and a delicious aroma of new bread wafted out onto the slum street. Lizzie's stomach rumbled.

Longing to taste fresh bread, she slowed at the window and glimpsed in. Several loaves were on the counter, steaming in the cold air. Plucking up courage, she decided to rush in and steal one. Just as she stepped across the threshold the baker appeared from the back of the shop.

Thwarted, she moved on, disappointment welling up and bringing her close to tears.

Ahead, a man and a woman were stacking junk onto a rickety stall.

There was nothing but clothes and household items used so many times they were falling apart. With nothing to eat in sight, Lizzie passed by the pair.

It was further than she remembered to Arburton Street and by the time the corner of the road came into view, Lizzie was thirstier than ever, her mouth so dry her tongue stuck to the roof of her mouth.

All she could hope for was that the seamstress she was heading for would take pity and offer her a drink, even water would be good.

She wondered if this part of the town was even colder than back home for her feet were like blocks of ice and the cold fog had penetrated her clothes giving her goose-bumps every time she shivered.

To make matters worse, the hem of her black skirt had become damp and it swished the back of her ankles at every step.

To take her mind of her woes, she practiced the words she would use in her plea for sewing work. Lord help them if the woman refused, for there was hardly anything to eat last night and not much hope of any today if her words fell on deaf ears.

Panic began to rise in her, like swirling moths beneath her ribcage.

What would her mother and father say if she went back home empty handed, the consequences didn't bear thinking about.

She was so involved with the "what ifs" that she arrived at the dressmaker's shop without realising it.

Taking a deep breath, she focused her eyes on the bay window and the pretty gown displayed there.

The shop door wasn't for the likes of her, she'd heard this said many times in the past year or two so she headed for the back alley running at the side of the building.

Opening the tiny green gate leading to a small garden and the back door of the house, Lizzie, heart in her mouth knocked on the door with her cold knuckles.

Footsteps hurrying down a short hallway made Lizzie smile, for when whoever it was, probably the maid of all work, saw who it was knocking, she may regret rushing to answer the door.

The door opened wide and in an instant the smile on the maid's face died.

Looking down at Lizzie, she grimaced. "What do you want?"

Before Lizzie could answer, the young woman said, her lip curling slightly, "We don't want anything, thank you, so take your fleas muck and awful manners away from the house." She began to close the door but Lizzie put her hand on the door panel.

"I'm on an errand. My mother sent me to speak to the seamstress."

The maid sniffed loud in her nose.

"The mistress is busy."

Lizzie looked forlorn. "I only want to give her a message, then I will be on my way."

A bell rang in the kitchen. Tut-tutting with annoyance, the maid turned and went towards the kitchen door to attend to it.

Lizzie grabbed the heaven-sent opportunity and dashed into the house. Running down the hallway, she went through the open door of the shop.

The seamstress, wearing a black taffeta dress, was sitting by a meagre fire, the white cotton garment she was sewing was thrown across her lap. The elderly woman started to rise on seeing Lizzie.

"Who are you?" she said a little indignantly. "Why did the maid let you in?" She has instructions…"

"I'm sorry, Mrs Kemp," Lizzie said, remembering the woman's name. "My mam sent me."

Lizzie's foot covered its partner in an attempt to bring warmth to her toes.

To Mrs Kemp the child looked vulnerable, cold and hungry. She spoke kindly. "Who is your mother? What is your name?"

The woman's obvious kindness emboldened Lizzie and she said, "Me mam is Mrs Straine. She sometimes does work for you. She sent me to ask if you have some sewing that needs doing."

Mrs Kemp shook her head sadly. "I'm afraid not. Your mother's work leaves a great deal to be desired. I have received complaints from my customers, so I can't give your mother any more work."

Lizzie's eyes filled with tears, dreading the telling-off she would receive when she repeated Mrs Kemp's words. "Oh please, Mrs Kemp. I will ask her to take more care. I'm sure she could make a good job of whatever you sent her."

Before the lady of the house could reply, the maid came into the room and seeing Lizzie standing there—her dirty feet upon the just cleaned rug—was furious.

"I told you to go away. I said Mrs Kemp was too busy to see the likes of you. Now be gone before I clout you with the fire poker."

Her face red with indignation, she advanced on Lizzie, her arms flaying and attempting to land a blow.

Trusting her maid to get rid of the little ragamuffin, Mrs Kemp went back to her sewing.

Dodging the blows, Lizzie made a beeline for the door and ran down the hall and outdoors at breakneck speed.

Within seconds of leaving the warmth of the house, the soles of her small feet were slapping on the wet cobbles. She ran toward the slum she called home, tears streaking her dirty face, the hunger and thirst forgotten in her hurry to put distance between the seamstress and her bad-tempered maid.

There was worse to come, for when she reached home her mother was likely to berate her for not doing the simple job of asking for work and getting it.

It would be her fault the family went without dinner tonight.

Her father, if he had sobered up and was awake, would harangue her for letting everyone down. Without a thought to his own blame in the matter.

"It's not fair," she blurted out as she ran.

An old man on the street corner laughed out loud on hearing her. "Bit young to be talking to yourself," he chortled as she ran by him.

Giving him a withering glance, which seemed to make him laugh the harder, Lizzie went faster hoping to leave him and her other troubles in her wake.

Ahead was the house her family shared with many other families, and in the cramped and smelly room they shared with the Watsons, her mother and father would be waiting.

In a quick sprint she went up the dirty steps and through the front door. At the top of the stairs she paused, and then made her way to a closed door. Behind it her parents would be waiting.

Taking a deep breath, Lizzie grabbed the doorknob to open the door. The knob turned but the door was locked. Never in her young life had she known the door to be locked. There were too many people and too many comings and goings for it to be practical to lock the door.

She tried again but the door didn't budge. Panicking, Lizzie banged hard. There was a small scuffing sound coming from within the room but little else.

"Let me in, Mam," she shouted.

There were no arguments going on between her sisters, no sound of her father's deep snores, or her mother pleading for a bit of peace and quiet.

"Let me in," Lizzie shouted again. Kicking the door with her foot.

The door opened a fraction and a strange woman put her face into the gap. "Go away," she hissed.

"I can't go away. I live here," Lizzie cried angrily.

"Not any more. Your family have moved out. I suggest you follow them."

Raw panic rose in Lizzie and she gulped air. "What do you mean, they moved out? Where have they gone?"

The woman behind the door began to pull it closed. "Don't know and don't care. The room belongs to us now, so you cannot come in. Go away."

"I beg you," Lizzie cried. "Let me in to see for myself."

The door banged closed.

For long minutes Lizzie stood looking at the chipped paint and scuff marks on the wooden door.

Suddenly it came to her that they would not have gone far without her. Galvanized by the idea she ran back down the stairs and started knocking on the other doors in the house, banging frantically when no one answered.

It was a wide-awake nightmare, and she turned from door to door begging those inside to tell her where her family were.

"Mrs Johnson, can you hear me? Do you know where my family is?" Mr Taylor, answer the door. Someone please tell me. Where are they?"

Several minutes went by and Lizzie sat on the stairs crying into her skirt. "Where are they? Someone please tell me," she wailed, screaming into the long hallway.

Eventually Mrs Johnson's door opened. "Lizzie Straine. it's no good carrying on like that," the old lady said poking her head out.

Lizzie came upright and flew to the old lady. "Mrs Johnson, I can't find my family."

A loud sigh escaped the woman's wrinkled and dry lips. "They've gone, Lizzie."

"But why? Where?"

She sighed again. "They were evicted by the landlord. Your father had not paid the rent and so the family were thrown out."

"They'll come back for me?" Lizzie said quietly.

The woman didn't answer.

"Perhaps they are staying nearby, with a friend," Lizzie said hopefully.

The woman shook her head. "What friend? Your Mam is too downtrodden to have friends and your father…"

"What about my father?" Lizzie said, her eyes narrow and voice sharp.

Mrs Johnson sighed again. "Your father is too rough when he's taken drink. Folk don't trust him. it's unlikely anyone has taken them in."

"Can I stay with you until I find them?" Lizzie's eyes pleaded.

The door began to close and then all Lizzie could see of Mrs Johnson was a sliver of her dirty black dress and grey shawl where it tied at the front.

"I haven't room. My husband wouldn't want a stranger in here."

Lizzie put her hand on the door to prevent it closing completely. "But I'm not a stranger, Mrs Johnson. You have known me since I was born."

The door closed entirely as Lizzie heard the woman harrumph "More's the pity," and retreat back into the sanctuary of her messy room.

At a loss of what to do next, Lizzie went outdoors and began to bang on the doors of the adjacent houses but she learned nothing of the whereabouts of her family.

Now she was seriously missing her mother and every few moments she swiped her eyes with the back of her hand to stem the tears.

Eventually evening began to fall and the temperature which had hardly risen all day plummeted. Lizzie was cold and hungry.

With nowhere else to go, and hoping against hope her father would find her, she curled up on the back step of her old home.

With her back against the door, Lizzie waited for morning, or a miracle.

Chapter Two

As the daylight disappeared, and dusk arrived, night bats swooped around the house, and Lizzie had covered her head with the shawl to stop them flying into her hair and getting entangled there.

Her sisters said such an occurrence was nonsense, just an old wives tale. But in the dark hours, as the little shadows swooped and soared, Lizzie was afraid it may be true.

The night was the longest Lizzie had ever lived through.

Every minute seemed like an hour. It was cold, and with nothing but her frock and an old shawl that was once her mother's to protect her from the freezing night, she spent the time shivering and hungrier than ever before.

Lizzie had often gone without supper, but generally there was something on the table every day, and Lizzie hadn't eaten since the day before her mother had sent her out to Mrs Kemp.

At first light, just as the sky was changing from ink-black to dark grey, Lizzie realised that no one was coming to find her. If they were, they would have discovered her here at her old home.

It came as a terrible blow to know her family had abandoned her. She couldn't think what she could have done for them to even consider doing so. *Had her mother sent her off to the seamstress so the family could run away without her?*

She loved her mother and found it hard to accept her mother had no love for her and had thrown her away like an old piece of junk that was no longer required.

Lizzie cried her heart out. Tears spilled from her eyes and ran down her tiny, thin face, leaving clean tracks, against the grime that clung to her. In this new dawn Lizzie's heart began to harden against the people that had treated her so cruelly.

Somewhere amongst the rickety roofs a pigeon cooed and then another answered.

The tiny sound stirred Lizzie to movement. Standing up, shaking out the deep creases in her skirt, she tightened the shawl around her shoulders.

First she would go to the public midden and relieve herself and then walk to the water pump and swill her face and hands and also take a drink. The water would fill her belly for a little while until she could find or steal food.

Moving made her feel a little better. She had no plan but hoped that one would come to her soon. There was no point in waiting for something to happen.

There was no help here, she had been abandoned not only by her family but the neighbours too. People she had known all her life.

They, like her, were as poor as church mice and had nothing to share but a smile and a friendly word, so she would not think badly of the poor folk.

The midden, a six-holer on Rotherman Street, was empty when she got there.

Letting herself in, wrinkling her nose against the stench of the place, she lifted her skirt and relieved herself as quickly as she could.

Leaving the wreak behind, she went to the public water pump and sluiced freezing cold water on her tear-stained face and got as much of the muck off her hands as she could under the stream of water.

Reluctant to put her cold feet in the near freezing water she half closed her eyes against the agony and cleaned then as best she could.

One day she would have boots, warm and cosy against the chill of the cobbles. Combing her fingers through her auburn-brown hair she did her best to get rid of some of the tangles.

Colder than ever but a little refreshed she started to walk towards the markets and shops of the city. Her steps brought her to the docks and here she stopped for a moment to look at the yard her father was sometimes to be found.

For a fleeting moment she was tempted to go there but then she recalled his harsh words said more than once, when berating her mother, for the only living children, were girls.

"More's the pity the lad hadn't lived. He'd been more use than these girls."

Lizzie's eyes glazed at the memory of her father's accusing glare.

Harold had died only a few months after he was born when Lizzie had been a small child herself. She only knew of him from her father's rants, and that he would have gladly swapped her for him.

And now, because she was not a boy, he had left her without a backward glance, abandoning her at ten-years of age to her fate. No, she would not go looking for him and perhaps get a clout for her trouble.

Turning away, she tried to get the image of her mother out of her mind. It made her so sad to think of her, and miss her so very much.

The sun, or what could be seen of it through the murky sky, was trying to break through the clouds.

Several times Lizzie looked to it expecting at any moment, there would be a little warmth, and the chill creeping beneath her shawl would miraculously disappear. Her bare feet were freezing and with each step pain shot through them.

Passing a bakery, sniffing the aroma of fresh baked bread her empty stomach twisted with hunger. It seemed so long since she had eaten or swallowed a hot drink and she felt light-headed and faint.

Furtively she stood on the step at the bakery door and looked in and felt a blast of warmth from the fires heating the ovens.

A little afraid, she glanced around to see if there was a loaf close by that would be easy to steal. A deal table was close by and it was stacked with loaves.

Lizzie felt her stomach contract with hunger just anticipating the warm bread in her mouth. The temptation was too great and moving as slowly as she could she took a step over the threshold. Her hand was out, ready to lift a loaf, but just at that moment a man in a brown leather apron swung round from where he was kneading dough.

Grabbing a broom he swung it at her. Lizzie jumped clear and began to run, his curses ringing in her ears as she shot out of the building and landed on the cobbled pavement.

Winded and afraid, she did her best to run away, but for long moments the man followed her waving the broom and cursing her, and every other ragamuffin, on the London streets. After a moment he tired and turning he ambled back to the bakery.

Cursing and hitting the pavement with the tip of the broom handle.

Lizzie ran on, until she was too winded to run another step. Coming to an old stone courtyard, she crept in. There was no one about and there was no sound of anyone being close by. Grateful for the seclusion after the frightful chase, she sneaked across the yard, eyes peeled for trouble and went to a corner hidden in shadow.

In minutes she was curled in a tight ball, her shawl wrapped around her to keep out the bitter cold. Exhausted, she was asleep in seconds.

How long she slept she did not know, the light of the day had hardly changed when she was shaken awake.

Terrified, she jumped up and was about to run away when an old lady caught hold of her elbow and held her tight in a firm grip.

"Hold still, little one," the woman said kindly.

Lizzie stopped struggling but she was well aware of the woman's grasp and that she did not mean for her to run away.

"What's your name?"

"Lizzie Straine," Lizzie replied in a small voice.

"Lizzie Straine. I've not heard that name in these parts. You are not from around here, Lizzie?"

"No, I'm not."

"So tell me what you are doing sleeping in the corner of my old yard."

Close to tears, Lizzie answered, "I have nowhere else to go. I have lost my family and I don't know what to do."

"Bet you are hungry," the woman said, relaxing her grip.

Lizzie nodded.

The old woman sighed. "Come with me. I'll give you something to eat and then we can talk about what can be done."

The thought of food made Lizzie's mouth water.

"Follow me, Lizzie Straine."

Without question, Lizzie followed the woman through a rickety door and into a large old-fashioned kitchen. Lizzie looked to the blazing fire burning in the hearth.

Hanging above the flames on fire-jacks, black cauldrons were gently steaming.

The atmosphere in the room was misty with vapour from washing soaking in wooden water tubs.

Lizzie felt she could sleep for ever beside the burning fire.

The old woman went to a cupboard and brought out half a loaf of bread and a large piece of pale yellow cheese.

Lizzie caught the strong aroma of the cheese and her mouth watered.

Pointing with a bread knife, the old woman said, "Sit yourself down, Lizzie."

Cautiously, like a shy kitten, Lizzie came across the room to the deal table and sat on a wooden chair, her eyes on the hunk of bread being cut on a round breadboard.

Downing the knife, the woman said, "Help yourself, Lizzie. I'm not short of bread and cheese. I make both myself and more often than not it is the only food I have to offer."

She touched Lizzie arm. "You look perished, lass. How long have you been out on the street?"

"Since yesterday."

"What happened? Tell me everything, and I will see if I can help you."

Lizzie eyes were on the bread and cheese.

The old lady smiled. "Help yourself to food first, you looked clemmed. I'll make a brew. A mug of tea will warm you through."

Lizzie remembered her mother saying yesterday that she had no time to drink a mug of tea as she had to get to the seamstress's as quickly as possible. Perhaps what Lizzie had thought earlier was true.

Her mother had planned on her being away from the room when the landlord came to throw the family out. Had ma protected Lizzie by sending her away or had she abandoned Lizzie without another thought? Lizzie didn't know.

"Come on lass, eat a piece of cheese," the woman said, bringing Lizzie back to the moment.

Lizzie took a chunk of cheese and bit into it. Shyly she picked up a piece of bread and wrapped it around a bit of cheese and began to chew quickly.

The woman brought two mugs and a steaming pot to the table. Sitting, she waited for the tealeaves to brew before pouring it out.

Lizzie watched the steaming liquid stream into a mug. Putting aside the bread, she lifted the mug and took a tentative sip. She was half-way down the mug before she began to eat again.

Elbows on the table, mug held in her two hands, the woman drank slowly.

Between sips, she said, "Around here I am known as Granny Eliza. Perhaps because I had so many children and eventually grandchildren. Most of them have gone now. Some have moved away for work and had families of their own and I'm now a granny to God knows how many little ones. Two of my children, Bert and Joe, died in the last skirmish abroad. Sadly three, Bertha, Jack and tiny Albert succumbed to typhoid in the eighteen-fifty outbreak. I'm telling you all this Lizzie because I want to take away the terrified look in your eyes. You are safe here. There is nothing to fear from this very old lady."

Lizzie chewed another piece of bread slowly.

"If it is men you are afraid of because they have hurt you in some way, I can tell you there are no men here. My husband, God rest his soul, died more than a decade ago. Since then I have managed on my own."

"Soon after Sidney departed, I started to take in washing," she waved her hand in the direction of the wooden wash tubs. "As you can see I am busy. It is too much for one person but I struggle on. Though rheumatics has taken its toll on my hands which are always in cold water."

She turned one hand, and then the other over, as if to inspect the damage of the disease on her fingers.

Watching her, Lizzie drank the last drop in the mug.

Without asking, Granny Eliza refilled it and pushed the milk jug across the table to her.

"Thank you, kindly," Lizzie said politely.

Granny Eliza poured the dregs from the pot into her own mug. "You seem a nice girl, Lizzie. You're polite. Now you have eaten your fill, tell me what happened to you."

Holding firmly to her mug with both hands, Lizzie retold the tale of going to the seamstress and then returning home to discover her family had disappeared.

Granny listened without interruption.

When the story was told, Granny Eliza said, "How would you like to stay here and work for me? You can help me with the laundry and deliveries. Your legs are a lot younger than mine so you'll run back and forth with no trouble at all. I've no bed to offer you but you can have a blanket and sleep in front of the fire. You can have all you want to eat. What do you say?"

Lizzie's eyes grew wide. In all of her life she hadn't always had a warm place to sleep or all the food she wanted.

"I'm very grateful, Granny Eliza.", Lizzie stammered. "I'll do my utmost not to disappoint you."

The old lady grinned. "Good, then that is settled."

Lizzie felt a great sense of relief to have a roof over her head once more.

Though she didn't doubt the work would be hard, she was prepared to do anything as long as she didn't have to sleep outside again amongst the flying bats and sinister people roaming the streets at night looking for whatever grown-ups look for in the darkest hours.

On this first day, Granny let her nap on her own bed during the afternoon, it was obvious to her that the child was completely worn out and a sick child would be of no use to her.

As the day was drawing to a close, she lit the candles and then shook Lizzie awake.

For a moment Lizzie had no idea where she was. Panicked, she jumped off the bed in a hurry. Seeing the face of the old woman in the light of the candle she remembered all that had happened, a moment of sadness swept over her like a grey blanket without any warmth.

Granny Eliza spoke gently, "Come to the table, Lizzie. There's vegetable broth for supper. I made it while you were sleeping from a cow bone given by the butcher, a few carrots and parsnips, old potatoes and What's left of the parsley from my tiny herb patch."

There was an appetizing aroma coming from a steaming pot placed in the middle of the table. Lying beside the pot was a metal ladle and an uncut loaf on a deal breadboard, a long sharp looking knife besides it.

Two earthenware dishes and spoons lay on either side of the table and beside the loaf of bread was a short stubby candle in an old fashioned candleholder, the flame casting a golden glow across the board.

Lizzie was used to eating with a cracked dish balanced on her lap, and an old bent spoon to scoop up the boiled vegetables and thin stock, the stew usually undistinguishable from day to day.

Granny Eliza's table with its pot and dishes, spoons and ladle, wasn't something Lizzie had enjoyed during her short life and the neatness of it and the appetizing aroma made it more like a feast to Lizzie than just an ordinary meal.

Lifting the hot pot lid with a cloth, Granny Eliza dipped the ladle into the thick pottage and drew out enough to fill one of the bowls which she passed across the table to Lizzie.

The temptation just to start eating was great but guessing what was expected of her, Lizzie held back waiting until Granny Eliza had filled her own. Once Granny Eliza was settled with the full dish and a piece of bread for dipping into the mix, Lizzie picked up her spoon.

The taste was exquisite like nothing she had eaten before. Eating slowly, dipping bread in until it oozed with liquid, Lizzie relished every mouthful.

Granny Eliza, in celebration of her acquiring a new recruit had baked an apple suet pudding and unwrapping it from the cloth it had steamed in she brought it to the table. It was Lizzie's very first pudding and her eyes grew wide at the sumptuous sweetness of it..

Later, enjoying a mug of tea by the fire, Lizzie unburdened herself, telling Granny Eliza of Mrs Johnson's harsh words implying her father was a drunkard and a rough man when he had taken drink.

The old woman was wise enough to know that Lizzie's suffering over the past days was too great to burden the child with more opinions about her parents, and Granny Eliza kept her own counsel.

It was clear the man had to be an abhorrent, obnoxious nave for abandoning a child to her fate in the streets.

Stroking Lizzie's head as she sat on the floor before the fire, she said, "Mrs Johnson was not in a position to know the truth of the matter. Perhaps you will discover the truth for yourself one day. For now it is best to reserve judgment on those whose voice cannot be heard for the moment."

Lizzie was content with Granny Eliza's words.

Well-fed for the first time in her life, warmed by a blazing fire, she was soon asleep and dreaming of cattle grazing in green fields, a neat fence and a five-bar gate keeping them safe from harm.

Chapter Three

December 1875

It was barely light when Lizzie woke the next morning. Seeing the few embers in the ashes at the bottom of the grate, she threw off the blanket and stood.

Stooping to the wood basket she took out a few logs and placed them onto the tiny red dots. In minutes the new wood started to smoke.

Filling the kettle from the bucket of water by the hearth, she put it to the now smouldering wood. She would make Granny Eliza a pot of tea so the old lady could enjoy a few minutes peace with a brew before she rose to begin work on the dirty washing delivered by customers last evening.

While she waited for the kettle to boil, she topped up the cauldrons hanging from the jacks and then ran out into the yard to draw water from the well.

All the pots were beginning to steam and the bucket by the hearth had been refilled when Granny Eliza appeared from the tiny attic bedroom above the kitchen.

She was smiling, tying her shawl about her waist. "That is very thoughtful of you, Lizzie. I do enjoy a cup-of-tea in bed. My old Sidney used to bring me one, but I never had it again until you, Lizzie." Lizzie felt a warm glow, even though she he had heard it many times.

Coming to the fire, Granny Eliza was happy to see the cauldrons full of water and beginning to steam. "What a marvel you are Lizzie."

Delighted with the praise, Lizzie blushed a pale pink.

"I shall make toast," the old lady said. Turning to the table, she opened a small drawer and rummaged in the few utensils there. "Where's that toasting fork— it's in here somewhere," she said clattering the things together. "Here it is," she said drawing out the ancient, long fork.

"Get the loaf from the cupboard, Lizzie. We will have hot toast in a minute."

Going to the cupboard, Lizzie gave a thought to how at home she felt with Granny Eliza. Though the work was hard and she worked long hours, it was far better than having nowhere to sleep and hunger gnawing at her belly.

Bringing the bread and cutting board back to the table she put both down. Granny Eliza started to slice the cut loaf. With two thick slices cut she went to the cupboard and got out a basin of dripping. Sniffing it, checking it was still edible, she put it beside the bread.

"It's a bit of a bother toasting bread, but it's nice to have it sometimes, isn't it?" she said piercing a slice with the prongs of the fork and turning to the fire.

Putting the bread close to the reddening flames she watched it turning brown. With one side done she turned the bread and put it back to the fire.

It was done in a few moments and she passed it to Lizzie. "Spread some dripping on it while it is still hot. Eat it quickly."

It tasted so lovely, Lizzie ate it with her eyes shut to savour the flavour.

With the few things washed-up and the day's laundry sorted into piles, the working day began. Lizzie bailed water out of the cauldrons with an old tin jug and put it into the wooden tubs. Granny Eliza had shown her how to swish water and swish the linen sheets around the tub with a dolly stick.

It was hard work and soon Lizzie's arms ached with the effort, even after these months, but she said nothing to Granny Eliza as she was grateful for a roof over her head and food in her belly. Wringing out the clothes and putting bed sheets into clean cold water, Lizzie was soon wet through, her hands and arms red and freezing cold.

Granny worked as hard as Lizzie but expertise and strength made the job easier for her. Sitting with a mug of tea and a piece of cheese at midday cheered Lizzie, and she was soon ready for an afternoon of hard work.

Getting up from the table, Granny Eliza swept stray grey hairs off her face and tucked the strands behind her ears.

"Are you ready Lizzie?" she said cheerfully. "Let's give a final rinse to the sheets and then wring them out so they can go on the washing line."

Lizzie looked to the small window and to the grey clouds covering the sky.

Reading Lizzie thoughts, Granny Eliza nodded. "It doesn't look very good out there, but there's a bit of a breeze and hopefully It'll dry the sheets enough that we don't have to suffer them dripping water on us all evening."

She looked to the wooden racks suspended from the low ceiling. "It is horrid when the weather is too bad to hang out the washing. Drip, drip, drip until everything is damp or wet through."

"It was the same at my home," Lizzie said. "Everyone put their wet washing on the banisters and the stairs would be wet and slippery because they were so filthy."

Granny Eliza tut-tutted, wondering why the folk where Lizzie came from didn't take care of the house. She remembered her own mother trying to manage on her own with ten children to feed after her husband ran off. She eventually succumbed, took to her bed, and gave up. By the time she was thirty, with no one to take care of her, she was put into an asylum.

No stranger to poverty herself, she understood that destitution draws the life out of even the strongest people until they become incapable of taking care of the basics.

She glanced at Lizzie and thought of the poor child on the streets without even a crust of bread or a warm place to put her tired head.

She wasn't going to waste time thinking of the child's parents, abandoning her, not caring if she survived.

Terrible things happened to lone children, the orphans of the parish were too often victims of men and women's depravity.

"Come on young Lizzie," she said cheerfully to banish the ghosts that had invaded her thoughts. "We'll get the sheets wrung out and on the washing line. Nothing like washing billowing in a breeze to cheer a woman's heart."

Lizzie smiled. It was nice to be thought of as a woman.

Wringing out the clothes was a difficult job. It took strong arms, and although Lizzie worked hard, she needed to re-wring them several times. Already damp from the morning work, she was thoroughly soaked soon after midday.

Granny Eliza was right, Lizzie decided as she viewed the washing now pegged on the line and blowing ever so gently in the cold air. She did feel better, seeing the clean wash hanging on the line.

Going back into the ancient house, Lizzie set about filling the cauldrons above the fire and running to the pump to draw more water.

In the afternoon the fire was stoked up and Granny Eliza put the irons to heat near it. The table was cleared and an old blanket put across it and she began the daily task of ironing the laundry.

Darkness had fallen, rain pitter-pattered on the small windowpanes before Granny Eliza called for the working day to end.

Taking the old blanket off the table, she folded it neatly and put it aside. In minutes she had the pot of broth left from last night's supper heating in the bread oven.

Almost too tired to move, Lizzie sat on a wooden chair before the fire watching the flames, feeling some of the stiffness leave her tired muscles.

Granny Eliza brought the bread and breadboard from the corner cupboard and laid it on the table. The two earthenware dishes and the spoons were put either side of the table.

A routine was being set and Lizzie welcomed the change that had come to her life. Though she missed her mother and sisters unbearably, she had become attached to Granny Eliza. She still hadn't made up her mind about her father, but was beginning to doubt he was the man she had thought him to be.

Coming to the bread oven with a cloth in her hands, Granny Eliza drew out the heated pot and took it to the table.

"Come on, young Lizzie," she said. "Time to eat."

The food was as delicious as it had been on every previous night and Lizzie finished the meal by wiping out the dish with a piece of bread. The cheese was brought to the table and what was left of last night's pudding. Though she was already full, Lizzie made room for a little bit more.

When she was finished she rubbed her belly. "That was really good, Granny Eliza. I'm full-up."

Lizzie had never told the old woman she'd never had a full belly before Granny Eliza found her. It seemed like belittling her mother's attempts at feeding her family. A hard thing to do when there's little or no money coming in.

If he had money in his pocket her father was likely to take it to the local inn keeper and put it in his coffers in exchange for a belly full of ale.

With the few dishes washed and the table cleared, Granny Eliza said "I'm off to my bed, Lizzie," she said. "I'm worn out and I expect you are too."

"I am a bit tired," Lizzie said yawning loudly.

Taking the candleholder with the lit candle off the table, Granny Eliza made for the narrow and steep stairs leading to her attic bedroom.

Watching Granny Eliza as she made her way upstairs, Lizzie's eyes followed the light on the tan coloured wall until the door above close shut.

The light of the fire and the dancing flames gave a warm glow to the kitchen. Too tired to do anything but remove her frock and drape it over the back of a chair, Lizzie wrapped her blanket around herself and using her old grey shawl for a pillow, lay down by the hearth on the flagstones.

She was asleep in minutes but she awoke a little later with a sore hip and aching shoulders. Turning over she made herself a little more comfortable and fell back to sleep, dreaming she was in the room shared between ten people, listening to the sounds of the night made by four adults and six hungry children.

Outside, the ancient cottage and the courtyard was still and quiet but for the occasional call of a barn owl calling to its mate. There were many hours of darkness before the dawn broke the horizon, lighting the roofs of the city buildings to silver grey.

Granny Eliza didn't see the change from day to night, she slept on already accepting that Lizzie would be up and beginning her day, shouldering the load of work to be done.

Before six o'clock Lizzie had sorted the dirty sheets and piled them near one of the dolly tubs. The fire had been replenished with fresh wood. A kettle was warming on the metal hob.

The next job was to go out in the darkness and pump water into the bucket. It would take several trips to have the cauldrons filled and the tubs and tin bath for rinsing, topped with fresh water. Before she had finished the tasks, her frock and shawl were wet, and her bare feet frozen.

Bringing in the last bucket of water and putting it by the hearth, she wondered if she dared make a brew and sit for a moment warming and drying in the heat from the fire. From upstairs she heard Granny Eliza stir, the bed creak as she rose, and then, pee flowing into the pottery chamber pot. The kettle was coming to the boil, Lizzie began to prepare a pot of tea to take to the old lady.

It was later, after a breakfast of toast and a mug of tea, that Granny Eliza started inspecting the sheets to be laundered. Looking for stains that would need special attention to erase.

Coming across a yellowed sheet, she tossed it back down onto the floor.

"I'll need the blue rinse to get rid of the yellowing on that sheet," she said. "It hasn't been washed here in the past. I would never let anything leave this house in such a state. Bet it is Mrs Wandsworth's work. she's a slovenly laundress."

Tut-tutting she hunted in the basket of remedies she kept atop the corner cupboard.

"Can I look, Granny Eliza?" Lizzie said helpfully.

The old woman pushed the basket in Lizzie's direction. "There should be two dolly blues in there," she said.

Coming across the pair of tiny blue objects, Lizzie put them on the table.

"Oh, good girl. Your eyes are better for finding things than mine."

Granny Eliza tutted again. "That'll hold us up. It'll take a longer soak and rinse to get that horrid yellow hue from the cotton."

"Tomorrow, when you take the sheets back to the owner. You must mention the yellowing, and for the laundry not to be sent to Mrs Wandsworth's again."

Lizzie wondered how on earth she could tell anyone not to send their laundry to poor Mrs Wandsworth, whoever the lady was.

The hours of the days followed the same as the previous days. They soaked, washed, rinsed, wrung and hung clothes and linens; then ironed, folded and delivered them back in brown paper bags to their customers.

There was breakfast and a break at midday with bread and cheese and a stew or similar at night. And there was always a fire for the cold days, and tea to be had, and Sundays they took part of the day to rest.

It had been the best part of a year that Lizzie had been with Granny Eliza and despite the sadness for her family, Lizzie was content for the first time in her life.

Chapter Four

"It'll be Christmas before we know it," Granny Eliza said as they sat down to a plate of grilled fish at the end of the day.

Although Lizzie was never hungry like she had been before, the work was physically wearing, and Lizzie was as worn out as she had been the day before and the day before that.

She wondered how long it would take until she grew used to the hard work.

Pessimistically Granny Eliza said there would not be many days in the next three months where they could look forward to hanging the washing out and getting it dry. T

hey would need to get it out at daybreak so that it might dry as much as possible and then they would retrieve it when day closed in, and it might well drip on their heads for the foreseeable.

Lizzie didn't like the thought of it, but agreed with the old woman's prediction. Why only yesterday it began to rain so much that Lizzie had needed to run outdoors to retrieve the washing that hung limply on the line.

She had brought the laundry in where she hung it over wooden clothes maids, and watched it carefully, turning the clothes maids around every so often to make certain they would dry properly, in front of the blazing fire so it could be delivered on time..

The old lady smiled, "We have got through so much laundry these past few days, Lizzie. We will be able to afford a goose for Christmas. Perhaps some oranges too."

Such bounty was beyond Lizzie imagination and she looked to the old woman in awe.

"Friday, when you deliver the laundry to the customers, I want you to go into the butcher's on Beswick Street and ask him to put a bird aside for us. Just tell him Granny Eliza wants a plump fowl and not a scrawny one like he gave me last year. Be firm with him Lizzie."

Lizzie couldn't imagine being firm with anyone, least of all a butcher who was probably a big burly man who fed well and often.

"You could also tell him to put aside a piece of belly pork," Granny Eliza went on. "I'll make us a meat pie for Christmas Eve supper. Just like I used to make for my husband, Sidney, God rest his soul. Sidney came from a family of hard workers and there was never a shortage of food in their house. Not like my childhood home," she added wistfully. "There was nothing for Christmas or any other day. Life was hard in the workhouse but at least we were let out for Sunday school."

Lizzie couldn't remember ever celebrating Christmas.

It was a day her father and mother went to the inn and stayed there all hours. When they did make it home, they were always belligerent and spoiling for a row with the other families in the room. She and her sisters tried their utmost not to mention it was Christmas.

One year, the smell of the food cooking on the shared fire by the tenants in the room drove Martha to cry. The father had taken pity on the children and cut an apple and given them half each. Annie, hadn't been born back then.

She put the dark thoughts and memories aside and listened to Granny Eliza talk of Christmases past, when her children had been young and excited to open their presents on Saint Stephen's.

"Now you won't forget to tell the butcher to give us a plump bird, will you Lizzie?"

"No I will not forget. When I go to pick the bird up from the shop, I will check it for fatness."

"Good girl. I know I can rely on you, Lizzie, to do what's right."

Lizzie yawned.

"Listen to me going on about Christmas and you as tired as a child can be. Get ready for your bed, Lizzie. We can talk about this tomorrow morning."

Lizzie was grateful that Granny Eliza was bringing the evening to a close, she could hardly keep her eyes open and the pain between her shoulder blades was getting worse the longer she sat on the wooden chair in front of the fire.

Yet she counted her blessings, she was grateful for Granny Eliza for taking her in, otherwise she may have been starving and sleeping on the streets tonight in the freezing weather, or maybe a worse fate would have befallen her.

Sleep didn't come so easy this night to Lizzie. The flagstones on the floor were hard and cold. There was a draught coming under the door which blew towards the fire. With every gust of wind outdoors the temperature in the room seem to drop. Though she was tempted to put more wood on the fire, she didn't, instead she drew closer to the hearth as the room chilled off.

Her mind went to Christmas and she wondered if it was excitement at the prospect of celebrating the day that was keeping her from sleep.

Perhaps. In the back of her mind lurked dark and bad memories and as much as she tried to push them away, thoughts of a cold room and unhappy sisters with nothing, or little to eat, stole a sliver from the excitement of the plump goose, meat pie and oranges. She had been very angry with them at times, especially when they stole her food, but she knew they were hungry, as she had been.

But Lizzie wasn't hungry now and her conscience crept to chide her for the times she had pinched them, or yelled at them. Maybe one day, she might see them again, and maybe one day she might share a fat goose with them and maybe even an orange.

She had seen oranges on the market stalls and in the grocery shops at Christmas time but had no idea how they may taste.

Not even how they might smell, as she had never come close enough to smell the fragrance of the exotic fruit. Slipping into sleep, she wondered if Granny Eliza would manage to afford such luxury.

Friday dawned and the light at the window was a little brighter. Holding the blanket around her, Lizzie went to the window to look out. The courtyard was white with snow. The imperfections of the yard were hidden, the top step of the broken horse mount was softened by a layer of snow.

The cracked and uneven flagstones, laid more than two centuries earlier, were covered with a white gloss. Even the midden at the far end looked like an elf house with a draping of crystal white snow to cover the drab tiles. Lizzie was enchanted.

~ ~ ~ ~ ~

Next week it would be Christmas. And today she would go to the butcher and order the goose and also to deliver the finished laundry to the customers awaiting it. Dressing quickly, she ran to get the water from the pump giving little thought to her bare feet, they were already freezing cold from standing on the cold floor. She topped up the cauldrons and rinsing tubs with fresh water.

Back at the hearth, she lit the fire. It was time to make a pot of tea to take to Granny Eliza before the old woman stirred and relieved herself in the chamber pot. Pouring boiling water into the old teapot, she waited for it to brew and then poured it out, took a sip from her own mug and then went up the rickety stairs to Granny Eliza's tiny bedchamber.

Chapter Five

"Ah Lizzie, you're a marvel," Granny Eliza beamed as Lizzie delivered the tea to her.

While the old lady supped, Lizzie poured hot water into the tin bath and climbed in, using the soft soap in the glass basin to clean herself. She wanted to be very presentable today as she was seeing the butcher and delivering Granny Eliza's special message.

She rarely used the hot water to clean herself. Normally, she swilled herself under the cold water pump. It was wonderful, warming her to the bones, so much muck came off her. She washed her hair, swilling the suds out of it with warm water from the tin jug. She could so easily get used to such luxury, it was worth all the hard work just to get especially clean.

Drying herself on an old piece of linen she went to the fire to brush her hair dry. When it was done and she was dressed, she looked in Granny Eliza's small mirror she kept in the corner cupboard.

Her hair gleamed with hints of red copper and the face looking back at her was pale ivory, golden lashes lying like the tiny wings of a bird beneath her eyes.

Granny Eliza came down the stairs slowly carrying the used mug. On the bottom step she looked to Lizzie.

"Lord above, child. You are beautiful," she said slowly admiring the child. How old did you say you were, Lizzie?"

"I don't know," Lizzie replied. Perhaps ten I think, maybe eleven."

"Didn't your mother keep a record?"

"Not that I know of. She couldn't read or write, nor could my father."

"Hmmm, I think I could teach you your letters. I'm not very good but I get by."

"Is it very hard? It looks hard," Lizzie said. Granny Eliza was often telling Lizzie she was a marvel, but Lizzie wondered it that would extend to learning letters.

"It will not be difficult for a bright hardworking girl like you, Lizzie. We will start in the New Year. Until then we will have too much laundry to wash for folk. Especially the ones that have visitors coming over to stay for Christmas."

Excited by the thought that she would learn some letters, Lizzie smiled as she went to the cupboard and brought out the loaf of bread and basin of dripping. "I'll make the toast this morning. You take the weight off your feet, Granny Eliza."

Granny Eliza went to the door, "I'm away to the midden first." Opening the door, the old lady took a step back in surprise. "You didn't say it had snowed."

Lizzie smiled. "Slipped my memory. Must have been my excitement for Christmas.

The old woman chortled.

"It looks slippery underfoot," she said hanging onto the door frame before attempting to go onto the step.

"Hold on Granny Eliza. I will come with you to steady you," Lizzie said coming towards her.

Outdoors, Granny shuffled towards the midden, hanging firmly to Lizzie's arm, and watching her step carefully.

"Your feet must be frozen Lizzie," she said, noticing Lizzies bright red toes.

"I'm used to the cold. They do hurt sometimes though."

"I think I may be able to find something for your poor feet. There might be a pair of old boots or something left over from my children that will fit you. My children always had shoes, their father wouldn't have had it any other way."

"Lizzie thought of her own parents, and pushed then pushed the thought immediately away. It hurt to understand the truths that were gradually dawning on Lizzie."

When Granny Eliza was finished with the midden, they made their way back to the house.

Lizzie threw an extra log on the fire. "Soon as that heats up we can toast the bread."

Granny Eliza collapsed onto the chair beside the hearth. She shivered. "I hate winter, especially now I am old."

Even with the cold, Lizzie secretly loved the snow, especially when it sparkled with brilliant sunlight that made the piles of snow, glisten sliver-white.

Once breakfast was out of the way, Granny instructed Lizzie to go to the attic bedroom and bring the box under the bed down into the kitchen.

It was a struggle to pull the heavy box that was wedged under the bed, out. With the job accomplished, Lizzie carried it down.

"Put it here by the fire, Lizzie," the old lady said.

Lizzie did as she was bid.

Granny Eliza opened the dusty lid and brought out a brown coat and shook it out. "This was my eldest girl's coat. It may fit you, you've grown taller since you've been here."

Lizzie knew it was true, her clothes that had hung on her before were now snug, and Lizzie was almost half the way up to Granny Eliza's head now. Even Granny Eliza had said just a short time ago they'd have to see about some more dresses soon.

Jumping up, Lizzie tried it on. It wasn't a good fit, it was too large, but was warmer than Lizzie's shawl.

"There's a frock here," Granny Eliza said. "Perhaps the same size. But it may do."

Rummaging in the bottom of the box she pulled out several dusty and flattened shoes. "Try them on Lizzie and see if you can find something to fit your poor feet."

At the third attempt Lizzie found a pair of black boots that would fit her if she wore a pair of thick socks. She prayed there would be a pair of socks in the box that would do the job.

In minutes Lizzie had socks, a pair of boots, a dress that was too large, and a coat also too large.

"You'll grow into them," Granny Eliza said sagely.

Dressed in her second-hand clothes, Lizzie was ready to deliver the laundry to the customers and face the butcher and tell the man, "Granny Eliza wishes to buy a goose for Christmas and it must not be scrawny. It must be a fat one."

~ ~ ~ ~ ~

Carrying a flat bottomed basket stacked with brown paper parcels of clean laundry, Lizzie left the sanctuary of the house and made her way to the street running parallel with Granny Eliza's old courtyard.

Underfoot and on the roofs of the tenement houses the snow had settled. The cobbles of the pathway were completely hidden and Lizzie made her way cautiously as she was unused to walking with boots on her feet. The snow crunched and made a strange squeaking sound beneath the leather soles. She felt privileged to have a pair of boots and warm socks.

A few children passed her by with bare feet, red with cold and toes swollen with chilblains.

Though she did her utmost not to look at their frozen feet scuffing up snow, it was impossible not to glance down.

When the children had passed by and she had the street to herself, she threw back her head and opened her mouth to let the tiny flakes of falling snow settle on her tongue.

The air was cold, reddening her cheeks and her fingers holding the handle of the wicker basket.

Coming to the house of a customer, she checked what Granny Eliza had written on a bit of paper and made sure the number of the house matched.

Sighing, she thought how much easier it would be if she could read and knew at least a few numbers, and was glad that Granny Eliza had promised to teach her in the New Year. Though the task seemed monumental, it was worth the effort for she hated seeing something written down and not be able to understand it.

Making certain she had the right house, she went up the steps to the front door and lifted the brass knocker, knocking it against the door to make it's rat-a-tat sound.

Long moments passed and she was wondering if the house was empty when the door opened and a very old lady stood a little crookedly on the threshold. Her ancient eyes were almost white and Lizzie saw the poor woman was blind.

"Who is there?" the old lady said shakily.

Lizzie's voice rose a notch. "I'm Lizzie Straine. I have bought your clean laundry."

"I'm blind, not deaf," the woman said bad-temperedly.

"Sorry," Lizzie said a little more normally.

Putting the basket down, Lizzie took hold of the top parcel and shoved it towards the woman's hands. "Granny Eliza has sent your laundry."

"Thank you," the woman said a little unsteadily, taking the brown paper package.

"That'll be two-shillings," Lizzie said.

Slightly flustered, the woman turned and went back into the hallway and disappeared through an open door.

Waiting, Lizzie looked to the tiny snow covered garden, to the plants bent beneath the snow and showing only a few green tips.

A door opened and closed within the house and Lizzie turned her eyes to the hallway and saw the woman returning slowly. Reaching the threshold, she held out the coins and Lizzie took them.

As she couldn't recall the woman's name, she said cheerfully, "Thanks, Misses."

Tut-tutting and muttering under her breath, the woman closed the door.

Pocketing the coins, Lizzie went to the next house to deliver more laundry, thankful the basket was no longer quite so heavy.

With the third delivery, the lady of the house was reluctant to pay. Lizzie took the parcel she had just delivered from the woman's hands and put it back in her basket.

"I'll bring it back when you have the money to hand," she said calmly.

The woman gave a loud sigh. "Stay there," she ordered as she went back into the hallway and through what Lizzie supposed was the kitchen door. There was an altercation from within, a male voice raised in anger.

The kitchen door opened again and the woman came to the door and handed the coins to Lizzie while rudely snatching the parcel out of the basket, before closing the door with a bang.

Lizzie pocketed the money and went down the steps and made her way towards the butcher's shop, walking carefully on the snow covered cobbles.

Granny Eliza had told her to look out for a red and white stripped awning at the butcher's shop. Lizzie spotted the canopy as she turned the corner of the street and she made her way towards it.

Chapter Six

There were several dead rabbits, a dozen or more fowl their black feathers still glinting in the weak sunlight, and a brace of partridges strung up beneath the awning. Outside the shop doorway there were trays and boxes of vegetables Lizzie didn't recognise.

She tried to memorise the colour and shapes to ask Granny Eliza about them later. The potatoes, carrots and parsnips were easy to identify, she ate these most days. The little green things that looked like tiny cabbages, and the purple and white globes were new to her.

Parked in the wide doorway of the shop were several wicker baskets brimming with hazelnuts and walnuts. Hanging above these were little sprays of herbs, dark green, pale green and some silvery leaves. A barrel of red apples stood on the threshold. Inside, in the centre of the flagstone floor stood a table with a huge basket of oranges. Lizzie took a step towards it and sniffed the exotic fragrance.

A man behind the counter had his eyes on her. Lizzie guessed he was the butcher, he was as burly as she expected him to be, and wearing a bloodstained apron. He was holding a knife sharpener in his hand and a knife like no other Lizzie had ever seen, it looked fearsome and brutal.

Putting both aside, he came from around the counter. Bending to Lizzie to match her height, he said, "What can I do for you, little one?"

Lizzie didn't expect such a soft voice to come out of the mouth of a man his size.

Taking a breath, she said, "Granny Eliza wants a goose for Christmas. She said it must be plump and not a scrawny thing like the one you sold her last Christmas."

The man roared with laughter. "You tell Granny Eliza I'll have a very fat bird waiting for her on the twenty-fourth."

"Twenty-fourth?" Lizzie said with a frown.

"Christmas Eve, little one. Christmas Eve."

"Oh!"

"No, I've got a better idea. You tell Granny Eliza to come on the twenty-fourth at midday and I'll give her a tot of rum or two. She needn't carry the bird back with her. I'll drop it around to her home on the twenty third. Do you understand all that?"

Lizzie guessed that Granny Eliza would be pleased with the invitation and the promise of the bird being delivered. She gave the butcher her brightest smile."

"If you come with Granny Eliza, I'll give you an orange."

"An orange?" Lizzie said awe struck.

He laughed again.

Unable to keep the news to herself, Lizzie went back home quickly to tell Granny Eliza about the wonderful invitation.

Entering the old house, she found Granny Eliza ironing sheets at the table. The room was warm from the heat of the fire and the four flat-irons heating near the flames.

Flushed with excitement, Lizzie tumbled over her words as she told the tale of the invitation to take a drink with the butcher and the promise of an orange.

Granny Eliza laughed. "Hold on girl, I'm not hearing you plainly. Who invited who, and when?"

Eliza began again, "The butcher man has invited you to sup rum with him at midday on Christmas Eve. But better than that, he said he would give me an orange." Granny Eliza beamed. "I smelled one and it was so beautiful."

Granny Eliza face straightened. "What did he say about my goose?"

"He laughed, Granny Eliza."

"Laughed! Why?"

"No idea. He just roared with laughter. He's a funny man."

Granny Eliza, her eyes on the fold of the sheet, harrumphed. "I'll give him funny," she said under her breath.

"But isn't it wonderful about the orange? And the rum," she added as an afterthought.

Head lowered, Granny Eliza carried on ironing.

"I told him you didn't want a scrawny bird like the one he gave you last Christmas," Lizzie said off-hand.

Granny Eliza's face lit with a smile. "You are a marvel, Lizzie. Did anyone ever tell you that?"

Lizzie thought for a moment and then said, "Only you, Granny Eliza."

A tear came to the old lady's eyes. "What a pity. Thank the lord I came along."

"I thank him every night, Granny," Lizzie said quietly.

Putting aside the flat-iron, Granny Eliza kissed Lizzie's copper-gold hair.

Drawing herself up, she said, "When are we to collect the goose?"

"Oh, the butcher man said he would deliver it here on the twenty-third, whenever that might be."

"That's very kind of him," Granny Eliza said picking up the iron once more and beginning work again.

Lizzie was thoughtful and then said, "I expect he's bringing it because it will be very heavy as it is so fat."

Granny Eliza smiled. "I expect you are right, child."

The few days between the visit to the butcher and Christmas Eve couldn't go fast enough for Lizzie.

The morning of Christmas Eve she was awake before dawn tweaked the clouds. Rising off the floor, she folded the blanket and put it on the seat of the wooden chair Granny Eliza preferred to sit on.

Yesterday she had prepared so much, even stacking the wood close to the hearth so she could just throw it on the red embers that had survived the night.

The kettle was already filled, and she put it to the smouldering wood. The two mugs were on the table alongside the tin of tea leaves and the old brown teapot.

Going to the far windowsill, she took the milk jug from its usual place. The window was cracked and the frame rickety, so this was the coldest place in the room.

Hoping for snow, she parted the flimsy curtains and looked out. There was no snow but the yard was white with frost and the water pump had changed to a strange white apparition in the greying morning.

Excitement welled up and she grinned. Today she would go with Granny Eliza to the butcher's shop and get her orange.

Going back to the fire, she threw another log onto the growing flames. Putting her coat on over her shift, and pushing her feet into the second-hand boots, she went to the back door and let herself out quietly so as not to disturb Granny Eliza still sleeping upstairs.

The air was freezing cold and it bit into her already chilled cheeks. Running, but taking care not to trip on the undone boot laces, she headed for the midden.

She came out after a minute and went towards the back door, anticipating the warmth of the room beyond.

As the sky lightened to a dull blue, she saw a dark shadow, a mound, near the stone step.

Curious she went towards it and was surprised to find a mound of holly and ivy with a length of red ribbon placed on top.

Picking up the ribbon she took it into the house. The room was warm and inviting, the kettle beginning to simmer. Standing at the table, she took a moment to look at the scarlet ribbon with its neat edges and satin finish. It was beautiful.

Making the pot of tea, she looked to the ribbon several times imagining a small piece of it in her hair. But where had it come from? Stirring Granny Eliza mug of hot tea, she hoped the old lady would shed light on the mystery.

Going up the stairs, she was careful not to tread on the squeaky step.

"That you, Lizzie?" Granny Eliza called from her bed.

Lizzie smiled. It was a question the old lady asked most mornings as Lizzie approached. It amused her to wonder who Granny Eliza imagined it might be.

They had never had a visitor in all the months she had been here. Perhaps it was a ghost. Someone from long ago that Granny Eliza hoped for.

"Yes. it's me, Granny Eliza," Lizzie called back.

Coming into the room, seeing the old lady propped up in bed, the blanket under her chin, Lizzie put the mug into her ancient hand as it snaked out from beneath the grey bed covers.

"Thank you, Lizzie. You are a kind girl."

She smiled showing the gaps where her teeth were missing. "No work today, Lizzie. What a marvel. We can relax and enjoy the day."

"At midday we have to go to see the butcher," Lizzie reminded her.

"Oh, I haven't forgotten. He mentioned it yesterday when he brought the fat goose." She tittered.

"What's funny?" Lizzie asked with a frown.

"You are funny, Lizzie."

"Have you been outside yet, Lizzie?"

"Yes, there was a mound of holly and ivy. Also a red ribbon."

The old lady smiled. She was silent for a moment and then she said softly, "So he hasn't forgotten."

"Who hasn't forgotten, Granny Eliza?"

There was a happy smile on the old lady's withered lips. "Just an old, old friend," she said, her eyes shining.

Going back downstairs Lizzie went to the table and picked up the red ribbon. Knowing it held a secret, a happy secret.

Eventually Granny Eliza came down the stairs in a blue dress Lizzie had not seen before. Her silver grey hair was caught up in a bun that rested in the nape of her neck. She looked lovely and years younger than she did normally.

"Granny Eliza, you look lovely."

"Thank you, Lizzie."

Looking at the child's dress, altered so it at least fitted her, the old lady said, "You too look lovely. The dress is grand now it fits you properly."

Going to the door, she looked out and then down to the gift of holly and ivy. "I'll be back in a moment, Lizzie. Then we can decorate this old room and make it look fit for Christ's birthday."

They were busy until almost midday, and Lizzie marvelled at the splendour of the garland Granny Eliza fashioned and tied to the centre beam of the ceiling. Making a big red bow of the ribbon, she hung it from the centre. Lizzie had not noticed that a length had been cut off it and was now in the old woman's pocket.

Twelve o'clock struck on the old clock standing in the corner of the room.

Granny Eliza looked to the brass face. "It is always slow, always was," she said resigned to the problem.

"Time to put our coats on Lizzie. The butcher will be waiting."

Excitement bubbled up and Lizzie felt little moths fluttering beneath her ribcage. What if the butcher forgot his promise of an orange? She voiced her concerns to Granny Eliza.

"He will not have forgotten his promise Lizzie. I can assure you of that. Ted is trustworthy and a good man."

Happy with this, Lizzie opened the door and they went out together. Lizzie hanging onto Granny Eliza's arm to steady her on the flags slippery with frost.

Coming to the shop, Lizzie saw the awning was now down and a few game birds and a rabbit were lying on the counter within. The butcher was no longer wearing a bloodstained apron, he was dressed in a black frock coat and trousers, a cream shirt and a blue necktie tied with a flourish at the collar.

With a beaming smile, he came straight to the old woman as she came through the door. "I'm so pleased you could come, Eliza," he said kissing her cheek. "And your little friend is with you. What a treat to meet the child again."

He chortled. "She amused me so much, I tittered for days after her comment of the scrawny bird."

"She has her moments," Granny Eliza said with pride. "Lizzie often amuses me too."

"Come into the parlour. There's a good fire burning there. I'm expecting one or two friends and my favourite customers. They will be here soon for a tot of rum or two."

Lizzie was awestruck at the sumptuous furniture and draperies of the parlour. In the corner was a Christmas tree decorated with baubles.

"Oh, I see you've taken to the new fashion of a tree in the living room," Granny Eliza said cheerfully. "It does look rather splendid."

"My two daughters insisted on it. Since Prince Albert supports the fashion they thought they must too," he chortled again.

Handing a glass of rum to Granny Eliza, he looked down at Lizzie. "I recall I promised you an orange, young lady," he said beaming at her.

Going to the piano he took an orange out of the glass bowl there and handed it to Lizzie.

Instinctively, Lizzie put it to her nose. "It smells wonderful," she said eyes bright with enchantment.

"Thank you so much. This is my first orange and I will treasure it until I eat it," she said happily.

Granny Eliza and he looked down at her both beaming. The door opened and more people came in.

A while later, after Granny had supped two glasses of rum and her face was a little pink, she suggested they should return home as she was expecting a guest during the afternoon.

Lizzie was intrigued. Granny Eliza had made no mention of a visitor until this moment.

"Come, Lizzie" she said cheerfully.

As soon as the goodbyes and Christmas greeting were over and the butcher was thanked for the rum and the orange, Lizzie and Granny Eliza came out of the shop and onto the street.

Chapter Seven

A biting wind was blowing and there was a fresh layer of ice underfoot. Snow clouds had amassed overhead and the light was growing dim.

Granny Eliza shivered and buried her neck into her coat collar.

"Let me take your arm," Lizzie said. "The cobbles will be slippery."

Ahead, on the corner of the street, a small choir of children were singing carols. A man with them, wrapped in an enormous green muffler, was holding a lit lantern aloft and the light glowed amber on the children's upturned faces.

People braving the winter weather, their long coats and capes billowing in the wind, were shopping at the few market stalls remaining after the earlier market.

The door of the Jolly Roger inn was open. As they passed by, they felt a blast of heat from the massive fire burning within.

A fug of pipe smoke, ale and rum seeped into the cold outdoor air. They caught a blast of the noise of the crowded room. A few steps on and it was quiet again with just the thud of their boots on the brittle surface of ice lying on the cobbles.

Lizzie had never visited anyone before and the encounter with the friends of the butcher had been exciting and she was happy it was Christmas and she was with Granny Eliza.

Her mind flashed to her poor sisters, probably stuck in a room somewhere, their parents supping gin in a local hostelry.

She hoped that it wasn't so and her father and mother were taking care of them, but in her heart, Lizzie knew that was not true.

Determined that bad thoughts and memories would not ruin this day, the very best so far, she shoved aside the black cloud that always descended when she thought of her family.

"You have gone very quiet, Lizzie," Granny Eliza said softly.

"Not really. I was just listening to the children singing," she lied.

"They do have pretty voices."

"Yes," Lizzie said wondering if she could sing out loud.

Granny Eliza looked to the sky. "It'll snow before morning," she said. "I hope the goose fits in the oven. I would hate to have to trudge through the snow to the baker's and cook it in his big oven."

"Should have got a scrawny one like the one last year. It would fit then."

"Lizzie, you are a funny child."

Smiling, Lizzie put her hand in her pocket and felt the waxy skin of the orange and wondered if it was better to eat it today, or savour it until the morrow.

Arriving home, Lizzie went straight in and put wood on the dying fire. Granny Eliza took her time to take off her coat, straighten her hair and rearrange the bun.

"I shall put up the hoop. I know it is now considered old fashioned, but I like it."

"Where is it? Can I fetch it?"

"Yes you can, Lizzie, Your legs are a lot younger than mine. It is in the cupboard upstairs."

Lizzie ran up two at a time. She was back in no time with the old hoop in her hand.

Granny Eliza brought out a little box of decorations and began to tie them to the frame. It was done quickly. Admiring it when it was hanging in the window, Lizzie saw there was a tiny parcel wrapped in white paper and she thought it may have her name on it. The excitement was hard to bear.

The pork pie was put on the table and a bottle of port was fetched from the back of the cupboard. With a plate of little mincemeat pies Granny Eliza had baked the night before, the table was ready for the mysterious guest.

By three thirty in the afternoon, snow was falling steadily. Lizzie went backwards and forwards to the window to look out. Granny Eliza sat worrying that her guest would not arrive with the weather deteriorating fast.

At four o'clock a knock sounded on the door.

Granny Eliza came out of her chair quite spritely, and smiling, she went to answer the summons.

Sitting by the hearth, ears honed into the conversation, Lizzie awaited for the visitor to enter the kitchen.

An older man, quite good looking for all of his age, followed Granny Eliza into the kitchen. "This is Tom, Lizzie. He's an old friend of mine. With a nod of her head in the direction of the table, Granny Eliza signalled to Lizzie that she should pour out the port.

Tom accepted the port as Lizzie handed it to him, and smiled broadly at her. "You must be one of Eliza's grandchildren."

Lizzie stammered, not knowing, really, how to explain her situation.

"She's just the same as my very own, Tom." Granny Eliza said. "She lives with me here now and helps me with the laundry. I don't know how I ever managed without her. Lizzie is a marvel."

Lizzie gave Granny Eliza a smile, and positioned herself on the floor, a little away from the two of them sitting by the fire. She listened as Granny Eliza and Tom laughed and talked and reminisced about the past. It seemed they had known each other for many years.

When it was time to leave, Tom buttoned his coat and braced himself for the harsh conditions outside. But before he left, he leaned over and gave Granny Eliza a kiss on the cheek.

When he had gone, and the door was closed, Granny Eliza pulled the curtains closed with a happy sigh.

"Who is Mr Flynn?" Lizzie asked, unable to contain her curiosity a moment later.

"He's a very old friend."

Lizzie sat silently looking into the fire, hardly expecting the conversation to grow.

"Before I met my Sidney, he was the man my family expected me to marry. I suppose I did too, but, things happened, and then I met Sidney, and Tom met his wife."

"The holly and ivy and red ribbon were presents from him?" Lizzie asked.

"Yes, he sends the same every Christmas Eve. He's a thoughtful person and very generous."

Lizzie sat silently digesting this information. The men she had grown up knowing were not kind and thoughtful to their wives. It was more likely to be a cuff on the ear from such men, her father included.

It gave her something to think about late into the night, when she couldn't sleep because excitement and questions were bubbling around in her head.

Chapter Eight

February 1878-1880

The winter was bitterly cold. Lizzie trudged out in the snow almost every Friday during January and February to deliver clean laundry to Granny Eliza's customers and collect their coins.

Granny Eliza had developed a nasty cold that had seemed impossible to shake off. Lizzie found herself doing the bulk of the work while Granny Eliza sat before the fire or remained in her bed. Lizzie was troubled by Granny Eliza's failure to recover and tried to help her whenever she could, going about her work uncomplaining. She was still grateful to have a roof over her head and food in her belly.

Easter came and with it warm sunshine and longer days. It was just what was needed and sitting on a chair in the courtyard whenever possible. Granny Eliza had begun to respond to the homemade medicine she showed Lizzie how to prepare.

Gathering the herbs from the herb patch, mixing and blending, gave Lizzie great satisfaction.

Her reading was improving and there were occasions when she could manage without Granny Eliza's instructions and instead, she would read the recipes from a dog-eared book that had once belonged to Granny Eliza's late sister.

The working days were long but with the improvement in the weather there was the bonus of seeing washing billowing in the breeze on the washing line and not dripping on the floor beneath the wooden racks hanging on the low ceiling in the kitchen.

Granny Eliza was grateful for Lizzie's help, the winter would have been disastrous without Lizzie taking the brunt of the labour and bringing money into the house. After much thought, she decided it was time to pay Lizzie a small wage each week.

As the weeks passed and the weather warmed Granny Eliza recovered but she wasn't as energetic or healthy as she had been. More work had fallen to Lizzie and at the end of each day she was exhausted, often falling asleep sitting on the wooden chair by the fire in the early evening.

Granny Eliza was no longer able to stand for long periods of time to iron, so that chore now also fell to Lizzie. Fridays were the highlight of Lizzies week. On Fridays she went out to deliver the laundry to the customers. Sometimes she was able to enjoy a chat on the doorstep for a few moments before she hurried off to another customer.

The summer seemed to come to a sudden close, with no lead into autumn. The weather changed rapidly. Lizzie was faced with wet days where it seemed to rain from morning to night and they were back to suffering the washing drip, drip, dripping, on the flagstone floor.

Granny Eliza recognising how hard Lizzie was working gave her a few more coins every week and Lizzie kept a small stash of money in the top of the cupboard in the kitchen.

It built her confidence to know she had savings and should something dreadful happen and she was once more without a home, she would have time to find work and get a room before falling into destitution.

The following Friday, after she had finished her deliveries, she went to the second-hand stall in the market. She was lucky and found a good quality green wool skirt, a black coat and a pair of black button boots. Delighted with her purchases, she went home to show Granny Eliza.

Finding the old lady cooking a cow bone and making a vegetable stew took Lizzie back to that now far off day when she had come into the house for the first time and sat at the table to the first substantial meal she had in her short lifetime.

It seemed impossible that she had grown into a healthy girl with flesh on her bones instead of the scrawny waif she was back then.

She had a lot to thank Granny Eliza for and with tears in her eyes she kissed the old lady on the cheek.

Putting aside the spoon she was stirring the broth with, she said, "What's that for?"

Lizzie smiled and hugged her close. "For taking care of me and making me strong."

"Oh, that." Granny laughed. "It was nothing."

Lizzie laughed with her, remembering how as a child she always had something to say.

"It will soon be Christmas again. "Do you remember the butcher and the scrawny goose," Granny Eliza said smiling.

Lizzie laughed. "Yes, of course I do. I remember him laughing so loudly he could have frightened his customers away."

"He gave you an orange. Do you remember that?"

"Oh indeed I do. It was the first orange I had ever tasted, and Granny Eliza, you cut a length of red ribbon for my hair that Christmas. The ribbon was a gift to you from Tom."

Granny sighed. "I hope he makes it again this year. We are not getting any younger. He is two years older than me."

"Let's hope he makes it again. We would miss him." Lizzie looked wistful. "Why did you not marry him after he was widowed and you too were on your own?"

Granny Eliza sighed again. "Because he was always in love with his wife. Though she had died, he never let go of her memory."

"Sad."

"Yes, but it meant he had been happy with her for many years."

"I suppose so. But it is still sad."

"Aye. I suppose it is." She put the spoon into the pot and gently stirred. "This is ready if you want to eat, Lizzie."

"Yes, please Granny Eliza. I'm starving."

"You always are, Lizzie."

~ ~ ~ ~ ~

In the kitchen, the floor was wet from a recent load of washing that had been rinsed and was now sitting in a tilted wash tub where the excess water was draining off.

Outdoors drizzle was falling from a grey sky, veining the small window pane with dribbles of rain.

Lizzie looked to the window. "Will it ever stop raining?" Lizzie said, cutting up a strip of neck of lamb ready for the stewing pot as Granny Eliza scraped carrots, peeled an onion and cut them into thick slices

Granny Eliza's looked over to the wet washing, anticipating another evening of cotton sheets dripping from the laundry racks. "We've got our work laid out, getting these sheets dry. We had a visitor whilst you were at the market this afternoon."

Lizzie looked up from cutting the meat. "Oh! Who?"

It was young Adam Treadwell. He brought a note from his mother. They live on Albert Street. In the note it asks if we could do the Treadwell laundry." Granny Eliza's eyes flicked over to the full wash tubs. As Lizzie took in the sight, she murmured, "that's a big pile, that is."

Granny Eliza stopped scraping the carrots. "I know a new customer means more work Lizzie, but as the widow Mrs Arbuckle has passed on, we've lost her custom. Mrs Treadwell, as long as she hasn't got a great pile of dirty washing every week— will make up for the loss of Mrs Arbunkle's."

Lizzie cut through another piece of meat and tossed it into a basin with the dregs of salted flour in the bottom.

"It makes sense, Granny Eliza," Lizzie nodded, "it isn't only Mrs Arbunkle's laundry. The Smith family are moving from the district. That's three pairs of sheets and assorted odds and ends we will lose."

Granny Eliza put the scraping knife down. "I didn't know the Smiths were going."

Lizzie glanced at her. "Hugo Smith has a new job in Manchester. Seems it is an improvement from what he's doing."

"Well, I wish them luck. Times are hard, what with the skirmishes and what not going on in the world at the moment."

Lizzie smiled to herself. Granny Eliza read a newspaper when she could get her hands on one. Often the news she got was long out of date.

Crossing from the table to the fire, Lizzie threw the meat into the sizzling skillet. "I will go and see Mrs Treadwell, tomorrow."

A veil of blue smoke rose from the pan and disappeared up the wide chimney.

Granny Eliza's eyes went to the smoke. "Is that pan too hot, Lizzie?"

"No. It is fine."

Lizzie stirred the pot.

Granny Eliza decided not to interfere and went on with her conversation "Treadwell's won't be far out of your way. Mrs Treadwell lives quite close to Mrs Derbyshire. Tomorrow you will be delivering to the Derbyshire household."

Lizzie put the lid on the skillet and moved the pot to the back of the fire.

"Just hope it doesn't rain again tomorrow. I'm truly fed-up with the weather," she said making sure the lid was on properly.

Granny Eliza began to peel a few potatoes. "I know what you mean."

Earlier in the day the butcher had sent a few newspapers for Granny Eliza. Though several days old she was looking forward to sitting and reading after supper, as long as her ancient eyes could cope with the small print and the light of the candle.

With the potatoes peeled, Granny Eliza dropped them into the stew and settled it on the cooking jack above the flames. With a sigh, she went to the chair at the side of the hearth and sat.

"Shall I bring your newspaper, Granny Eliza?" Lizzie said setting knives and forks on the table.

"Please. I hope the news isn't only about Disraeli. I like to read about the queen too."

"After supper will you read it to me, Granny Eliza?" Lizzie said putting a newspaper into her ancient hand.

"Aye. I will. As long as me old eyes can manage to see."

Lizzie put four flat-irons to heat near the fire and then spread an old blanket on the table, and folded the sheets ready for ironing."

In the chair, lost in her newspaper, Granny Eliza read in the flickering firelight.

Eventually she dozed.

Lizzie went on with the ironing lost in her own thoughts, remembering the room she and her family once shared with the Watsons, dirty cramped conditions hardly fit for an animal.

She wondered how her sisters were now and where they may be. A part of her felt guilty for the good life she was living. The life her parents had unwittingly thrust her into.

What if they abandoned her sisters? Would her sisters fare as well as Lizzie had done? A fearful, angry ball rose in Lizzie's chest. No, they would be very lucky to survive at all. She pushed the thoughts away. There was nothing she could do.

The lamb stew was ready. Lizzie finished the last of the laundry in a hurry and put it on the racks to air. Putting the blanket back in the cupboard, she laid up the table for supper.

It was almost dark in the room, she had hardly noticed as she was used to working by the light of the fire.

Taking the candleholder off the mantelshelf, she put a spill into the fire and as soon as it caught she put it to the wick of a new candle. When the flame was steady she placed the candlestick in the centre of the table.

The room suddenly looked more cheerful.

Taking the skillet off the back of the fire, where it had simmered for more than two hours, she brought it to the table.

Granny Eliza stirred in her chair.

"Just in time," Lizzie smiled. "I'm about to put supper out."

Getting out of the chair, the old lady straightened slowly. "Did I nod off?"

"Think you did, Granny Eliza. The sleep will have done you good."

"I meant to do the ironing this afternoon. Never mind. I'll do it tonight," she said sounding resigned.

"No need. It is done," Lizzie looked to the drying rack beneath the ceiling.

"Oh Lizzie. You are such a good girl. I don't deserve such an angel."

"Now come to the table, Granny Eliza. We can start supper."

"Hope you are not too tired to read the paper to me, later," Lizzie said with a smile.

"Course not." Granny Eliza put a piece of bread in her dish of stew and then scooped it out with a fork.

"There's more about the queen than Disraeli," she said with a grin.

Lizzie cut a slice off the loaf of bread. "Good. I look forward to knowing how the lady is."

For several moments they ate in silence and then Granny Eliza glanced at Lizzie. "Young Adam Treadway seems very polite. He was neatly dressed and his boots were polished."

Lizzie smiled. "I'm surprised you notice. You don't normally have much time for boys."

"That's because most of them are dirty louts that can't do a job properly."

Lizzie knew that Granny Eliza was harking back to the lad she had paid to dig her small garden patch and he'd made a bad job of it.

"He was pleasant?" Lizzie tried to distract the old lady, knowing that if she didn't there would be a grumpy conversation about lazy lads.

"Aye. I liked him."

Leaving the conversation to lay quietly, Lizzie spooned up the last of the gravy at the bottom of her dish.

I'll wash the dishes and bank the fire before we look at the newspaper."

~ ~ ~ ~ ~

Lizzie took the still damp washing from the overhead racks, and pegged it out on the line. At least, it had stopped raining, although glancing up at the sky, she wasn't hopeful the weather would hold. She would need to get the fresh laundry delivered as quickly as she could.

Hurrying back inside, she untied the strings on her apron and folded it neatly on the back of a chair. Grabbing her coat she lifted the basket filled with brown paper packages in both of her hands.

"It is heavy. We did a fair amount of washing despite the weather. I'll be back as soon as I have delivered this laundry and called on Mrs Treadway."

She was halfway through the door when Granny Eliza called, "I'll have dinner ready when you get back. Take care, Lizzie. Cross the roads safely."

It amused Lizzie that Granny Eliza always reminded her to keep safe every time she left the house. She was thirteen years old now. Almost a grown woman and could take care of herself.

With the heavy basket settled on her narrow hip, she crossed the courtyard and went into the street.

After the seclusion of the house, the roadway seemed noisier than usual. There were several carts with tired looking horses in the traces passing in both directions, and two black carriages were bowling down the middle of the wet road.

A man standing on the pavement shouted at the driver of the first carriage, waving his hands wildly. "Slow down," he yelled at the top of his voice. "There are bairns about."

Ignoring him entirely, the driver sped on, splashing water up and over the hem of Lizzie's dress.

The pedestrian cursed and shoved his hands deep into his pockets, his shoulders slumped as he went into the ironmonger's nearby.

As she passed by the open door, Lizzie heard him bellowing to someone inside.

The heavy basket slowed her down, and she stopped now and again to flex her arms and shake the tingles out of her fingers.

With the deliveries made, and the customers" coins jingling in her pocket, Lizzie crossed the street and made her way to the Treadwell household.

The house was reasonably smart. The windows were clean and the brass knocker on the door polished to a shine.

Lizzie was just about to knock on the maroon door when it opened instantly and a boy, a little older than herself, came out in a rush.

Seeing Lizzie on the stoop, he stopped mid-step, at the same time forcing Lizzie to move backwards and stumble. Reaching out, he grabbed her forearm and steadied her.

"Oh! I'm really sorry miss-I didn't mean to run you down!" Lizzie brushed the hair back that had fallen over her face when she stumbled."

"Well, yer no worse than the carriage's on the road. They'd have ploughed me down if I weren't careful, and I dare say that'd been worse than anything you could've done to me." Lizzie felt the blush rising on her cheeks. "So I'm very well now, thank you."

The boy let go of her wrist and smiled, he had a fine looking face, with dark hair and blue eyes that were kind, and Lizzie felt the blush turn deeper. Turning his head over his shoulder he called out through the open door, "Mam, you're wanted." Giving Lizzie a quick nod, he stepped to the path and was gone in a moment. Lizzie's eyes followed him as he walked down the street.

"Ah, come in Lizzie, it is Lizzie isn't it? I'm Mrs Treadwell." Mrs Treadwell motioned Lizzie inside, and opened the door wide for her to enter.

"Just go right through to the left into the parlour and wait for me."

Lizzie took in the tiled floor of the small hallway and in the parlour. The modern whatnot in the corner of the room and the wooden shelves contained several little white plaster figurines and on the top shelf there was a brass oil lamp with a cranberry coloured glass shade. Everything was neat and tidy and it was obvious that Mrs Treadwell was proud of her home.

"Here we go love," Mrs Treadwell entered the room bringing with her a large pile of laundry. "I can't keep up with the washing any longer. Not since my mother came to live with us. She is an invalid now, and it's not just the washing, I can't leave her alone for long these days…. Still, you've got to look after your own, haven't you? She always looked after us."

Lizzie wasn't completely sure if Mrs Treadwell was talking directly to Lizzie. More than likely, it seemed she was speaking to herself about her situation, but Lizzie nodded her agreement and moved toward the pile of washing. Though there was more work than Lizzie would have liked to take on, with the loss of two of Granny Eliza's customers, she felt it must be done.

Lizzie folded the washing as best she could and stacked it in the laundry basket.

"Is that it Mrs Treadwell?" Lizzie said as she placed the final items into her washing basket. "I'll have it back by the end of the week."

"Good girl Lizzie. I'd have my son Adam help you carry it, but he's got a job of his own to get to." A satisfied smile crossed Mrs Treadwell's pinched face. "He's got a job in his uncle's warehouse. it's about time too," she said bitterly.

"Oh! Well I suppose that is very good news Mrs Treadwell," Lizzie agreed, not really knowing what else to say.

"Well, you've got to look after your own haven't you dear."

Lizzie moved toward the door. "I'll see you in a few days then." Lizzie said. Mrs Treadwell followed Lizzie out to the doorway and closed it behind her.

Walking back home, Lizzie wondered about Adam. She hadn't minded at all when he steadied her from the stumble, even if she had tried to sound gruff. She was just a bit embarrassed, that was all. But Adam seemed nice and even though she loved Granny Eliza, she didn't get much chance to talk with people of her own age. *Maybe I will see him again.*

Minutes before she reached the courtyard, it began to rain. Lizzie ran, the basket banging on her thigh as she went to rescue the washing she had pegged out earlier.

Arriving out of breath, she saw Granny Eliza, her skirt billowing in the coming storm gathering the almost dried washing and bundling it into a dry wash tub.

"Oh, there you are," she called on seeing Lizzie come through the open gates. Lizzie ran to her and unpegged the last pillow case, bundled it up and threw it on the wash tub and hauled it inside, then ran back and brought the Treadwell's dirty laundry inside.

Granny Eliza closed the door behind her, and they listened to the rain that had begun to hammer down on the tiled roof.

Pushing wet tendrils of hair off her face, Lizzie said, "That was lucky."

"Thank goodness we got it in in time," Granny Eliza agreed, "I didn't fancy another night of washing dripping on the floor. I'll hang this lot on the rack It'll be ready for ironing in the morning."

She eyed the wash tub filled with almost dry linen.

"We will have a bite to eat before we set about doing anything else," the old lady said going to the fire and stirring the pot.

Late that night, as the rain continued to pound the windows, Lizzie lay on the second hand straw mat she had found one lucky Saturday at the market.

Now, every night she rolled it out, and put it away again during the day. Although it was thin, it proved more comfortable than sleeping on the flagstones. And with old newspapers rolled under the gap of the door, the draft was kept out, and she was warm and cosy.

In the moments before she fell to sleep images of her sisters popped into her mind. She hoped they were not freezing and hungry.

One day, Lizzie promised herself, *when I can care for them, I will find them, and we will be together again.*

"Hello Lizzie," Adam Treadwell tipped his hat and nodded to her.

Lizzie was hugging a basket of freshly laundered clothing to her waist, balancing the weight of it on her hip. A faint shade of pink rose on her face. She smiled, happy to see him.

"Good day, Adam."

He smiled. "Are you away to our house today?"

"Not today, I will see your mother tomorrow though for delivery." Searching for something else to say, Lizzie declared, "She's very proud of you, you know."

"Is she?" he said, looking surprised.

"She told me you were working for you Uncle. *It's about time too,* your mother said."

Adam chuckled. Mam's a bit upset with my uncle, for all the money he has.

A puzzled expression formed over Lizzie's face, wondering why that was a reason to be upset with him. Being rich was a very good thing as far as Lizzie could tell.

"After my grandmother couldn't manage on her own and came to live with us, my uncle gave me a good job in his warehouse. He told Mam, that was his way of taking care of his own, but Mam thinks he took too long to do so.

Lizzie shifted the weight of the basket to the other hip.

"How far are you going with that?" Adam asked. "Can I give you a hand with it?"

The weight of the basket was heavy. It wasn't anything that Lizzie wasn't used to, but the idea of having the company of Adam brought a gladness to her and she felt her heart skip.

As they walked together sharing the weight of the basket between them, Adam told her about her uncle's merchant business.

As a younger lad, he had managed to curry favour with a well-to-do merchant by saving him from getting sorely fleeced in a criminal venture that was being executed from the docks.

In return, the merchant had taken him under his wing, and his uncle had learned the business of trading in cotton and silk and eventually married the merchants daughter. "

The thing is," Adam said, "it's his wife that the real problem. The likes of me and Mam and Granny aren't good enough for her, and Uncle, well – he just went along with it. I suppose it's the guilt that made him take me on.

Lizzie listened to his story, wondering what made even rich folk abandon their families. Her heart sank as she thought of her parents and wondered again how her sisters were faring.

"We're almost here. The Clarke house is the one with the holly hocks."

They reached the stoop and Adam sat the basket down.

He looked to the far end of the street and then said, "I must be on my way. I'm on an errand and I dare not keep my uncle waiting. I'm learning everything I can about the cloth trade and he won't be sorry he took me on." He smiled at her. "I'll see you again Lizzie. Maybe you can come to the park on Sunday, with a bit of luck the band might be playing."

Lizzie nodded her agreement. "I'll meet you there. What about 3 o'clock?" Granny Eliza would be reading her papers and nodding off in the chair by that hour on the Sunday. She wouldn't miss Lizzie for an hour or so.

He tipped his cap again and was gone in a flash and Lizzie watched him until he disappeared around the corner at the bottom of the street.

Chapter Nine

March 1880

Since Granny Eliza had first given Lizzie a payday, whenever she could Lizzie had saved most of the money, and she had a good hoard in a tin box in the cupboard, dipping into it to buy essentials when she was desperate for replacement clothes. She was growing fast and it seemed there was hardly any time between buying something at the second-hand market and then growing out of it.

Often on a Sunday, if Granny Eliza allowed, she would meet Adam and they would walk to the park. She was proud that she had caught Adam up in height and was now only a head shorter than he was.

"Actually you are a head and a neck, shorter - you only come up to my shoulder," he sometimes teased her.

She was thinking of this and smiling, as she scooped water out of a wash tub with a large enamel jug and took it outside to throw on the flagstones in the courtyard.

The dirty water splashed her boots and the hem of her skirt as she emptied the jug too quickly.

Impatiently she went back indoors and came out with another full jug and threw the water further away. Scum and soapsuds ran like a tiny fast flowing river back towards her boots and she stepped out of the way quickly.

Looking for a better place to dump the next jug of water, the tail of her eye caught a movement near the gate.

For a moment she thought she was seeing things.

Suddenly it became clear that she *had* seen something. And a woman stepped out from behind the gate.

Lizzie stopped and looked at the woman. Grey tendrils of greasy hair escaped the head shawl and moved in the breeze. Something about the woman was familiar, the shape of her face, the way she stood, the way her arms were crossed over her waist. Lizzie's eye's grew wide.

"Mama!" With a gasp of surprise she dropped the jug and ran, arms outstretched.

Sally Straine stood her ground. Flinty eyes watched her daughter running towards her.

It didn't register to Lizzie that her mother had not moved, and her arms remained locked over her torso. There was no loving expression in her eyes as she stared ahead at Lizzie.

In her haste Lizzie almost collided with her, instinctively she threw her arms around the woman and hugged her tightly.

The impact and the hard embrace squeezed the air out of Sallie Straine's lungs and she exhaled loudly.

Lizzie smelled the gin on her breath. She made no move to return Lizzie's embrace.

Bewildered, Lizzie took a step back her eyes fixed on her mother's face.

"You're grown up ain't ya Lizzie" her mother said.

Disappointment was etched on Lizzie's face and tears filmed her eyes.

"Mama," she said softly.

"You got yourself a cushy job, don't you!"

"I live with an old lady, Granny Eliza. I help her with the laundry she takes in, it is hard work, Mama. Not cushy at all."

Smirking, Sallie Straine looked to the overhead clouds. When her eyes fell on Lizzie again her expression was contemptuous.

"Well, it looks like *someone* is feeding you well."

Lizzie saw it was pointless trying to explain. Her thoughts now racing, her heart missed a beat suddenly sure her mother had sought her out to impart dreadful news.

"Mama, where have you been? Where are my sisters?"

Her mother paused for effect. Then her lips tightened and pucker lines appeared above her top lip.

"That's why I've come. it's your sisters that need your help. When you ran away you left them in a fine mess."

Lizzie's eyes widened and for a moment her mouth gaped.

Angry and amazed at the false accusation, she spluttered, "I didn't run away. It was you and Pa that did! Mama, you sent me to the seamstress. When I got back you had all disappeared."

Sallie Straine sniffed loudly and her lip curled. "You should have waited. We would have come back for you"

"Lizzie's voice rose and she shouted, "You didn't come back. I waited. I sat on the back doorstep and waited the whole afternoon and night."

Her mother shrugged her shoulders. "Well it doesn't seem to have harmed you."

"Harmed me! I had nowhere to go and no money to buy a bit of bread."

Sallie Straine brushed the tip of her nose with the back of her hand and sniffed. "It's a long time ago now Lizzie. No need to dwell on it. It is your sisters you should be thinking about."

"Why have you come mama? After all this time? And what about by sisters— you haven't answered my question. I asked you how they were."

Sallie Straine covered her grimy forearms with the grey shawl. Giving Lizzie a cunning look, she said, "They've grown now Lizzie, and it takes money to feed "em, keep a roof over their heads.....otherwise I have to turn them out into the world."

Lizzie was aghast. "But you can't do that. They may starve."

"They won't starve as prostitutes."

"Mama!" Lizzie cried out in horror. "You cannot do that to them."

"It is a matter of having to. We have nothing to live on. No money for rent or food. Your father refuses to feed the girls another day."

Her voice suddenly softened and she looked beseechingly at Lizzie, "Only you can save them Lizzie. Only you. Give me money for the rent and proper food and your father will let them stay a while longer."

Lizzie's eyes filled with tears. Without a coherent thought, she ran back into the kitchen and went quickly to the cupboard and took out the square tin where she kept her savings. Breathing heavily, she took some coins out and then ran back outside where her mother waited.

"Here have this," she said, thrusting the tin at her mother. "Promise me on your life that you will not let the girls go as prostitutes."

Clutching the tin to her breast, Sallie Straine said, "That's up to your father. We must rely on you helping us out when you can."

Without another word, she turned and with uncharacteristic fast steps went through the gate and into the street.

It took a moment for Lizzie to gather her wits. Lizzie ran out onto the roadway, but there was no sign of her mother.

How could she have disappeared so quickly

Sallie Straine had not gone far, she was hiding in an ancient porch of a derelict house. Her husband was with her. Taking the tin from her, he opened it and scooping up the coins dropped them into his filthy coat pocket.

He smiled wetly, the odour of beer escaping his mouth. He grinned. "Good work. We can come back for more again. Lizzie will not have given you her entire hoard."

Slipping out of their hiding place, they went towards the public house on the corner of the street.

~ ~ ~ ~ ~

Sad and worried, Lizzie threw a log onto the flames of the fire and stood looking into the flames, her mind in turmoil. In her heart she knew the money she had parted with would not save her sisters. It would go to fuel her mother and father's drinking habits. She had worked hard to accumulate the money and now it would be frittered away on gin and ale.

She felt her heart would break, not just for herself but her poor sisters, innocents likely to fare badly on the London streets, nothing more than prey for undesirables and the perverted.

How could she have been so stupid as to give her savings away? And why didn't she think to ask where her sisters were living. She felt violated, and stupid.

Next time her mother came begging, she would not get away without telling her exactly where the girls were living.

The rest of the day went in a blur, unable to concentrate on any task, she ironed throughout the afternoon, mindless toil she hoped would sooth her mind.

If she confided in Granny Eliza, the old woman would be furious that she had parted with her money so readily to a drunken woman who was capable of abandoning a child. She was embarrassed enough without Granny Eliza knowing how truly stupid she really was.

The day eventually came to a close, but not before Granny Eliza had asked more than a dozen times. "What's the matter? Why do you look so sad?" As she couldn't answer, Lizzie used the excuse she was tired. At the first opportunity Lizzie said she was looking forward to an early night and Granny Eliza gladly went to her attic room before eight o'clock.

When the old lady was settled, Lizzie unrolled her thin mattress and put it before the dying fire. Within minutes she was crying silent tears, afraid to disturb the old lady upstairs who would demand she was told of the problem.

~ ~ ~ ~ ~

Weeks passed by before Lizzie saw her mother again. It was a blustery day and Lizzie was hanging out the washing. Finishing the task she picked up the wicker basket to take back to the house when she spotted her mother watching from the gate.

Determined to get the truth out of her and discover the whereabouts of her sisters, Lizzie dropped the basket and strode towards her.

"You went off in a hurry last time I saw you," Lizzie said approaching her mother.

"I had the girls waiting for me," Sallie Straine lied.

It was hard for Lizzie to contain her temper. "Why didn't you bring them to see me?"

Sallie Straine tutted. "I didn't want a scene, Lizzie. No point you losing your job over a family problem."

"So why have you come this time?" Lizzie asked tight lipped.

Her mother looked to the flagstones. "The rent man is threatening to evict us, Lizzie."

Grabbing the sleeve of Lizzie's dress, she clung on. "You have to help us. Your father is too ill to work and there is no food for the girls. The rent has to be paid by tonight otherwise we are all out on the street. Your sisters will have to save us. Martha is past twelve years and Annie not far behind. Martha can bring some money into the house, though I'm reluctant to put her out to earn money to pay our rent, but it won't be long before Annie will have to join her."

She gave a long drawn out sigh. "Annie is prettier, so perhaps I should make her go instead."

Lizzie listened with growing horror picturing the innocent little faces of her sisters. "Can't father earn?"

Mrs Straine shook her head. "No. I told you he is ill."

She looked pleadingly to Lizzie. "You have to help us. Otherwise…"

She opened her arms and spread them wide. "The girls will have to find money."

Horrified, Lizzie said, "Where are they?"

"Who?"

"The girls of course."

Her mother remained tight-lipped and silent.

"I will not give you anything until I know where they are," Lizzie said firmly.

Mrs Straine sniffed and then reluctantly looked Lizzie in the eye. "We have a room on Justice Street."

"Justice Street, but That's not far away. Why didn't you say you were close by? I could have come to see my sisters."

Mrs Straine sniffed again. "Come on Sunday, Lizzie. If we pay the landlord, we will still have the room on Sunday."

Without a word, Lizzie turned and went towards the back door.

In the house, she listened for Granny Eliza's footfall but there was no sound and she guessed the old lady was taking a nap on her bed. Going quietly to the cupboard where she kept her coins, and taking several out, she went back outside to her waiting mother.

Before putting the coins into the woman's hands, Lizzie said, "What number on Justice Street?"

"Number fourteen," her mother answered, her eyes on the coins.

"We will look forward to seeing you, Lizzie. The girls will be so excited. They were interested in your job. They wanted to know everything."

"I'll be there at twelve," Lizzie said handing the money over.

Grabbing it, Mrs Straine shoved it into the pocket of her skirt. Without a backward glance, she scuttled towards the gate and went out into the street.

Lizzie strode to the gate and looked out onto the cobbled road but there was no sign of her mother.

With a long drawn out sigh, she went to the washing line and retrieved the basket. Sunday couldn't come soon enough.

~ ~ ~ ~ ~

Rising early on Sunday morning, Lizzie went to the window and looked out. Light cloud covered the sky, the breaks in it showed pale sunlight.

As it didn't look like rain, she decided to wear her new green shawl Granny Eliza had knitted especially for her. The colour brought out the copper tints in her hair, or so Granny Eliza said.

Re-lighting the fire, she put the kettle to boil to make a mug of tea for Granny Eliza.

At eleven-thirty, Lizzie left the house and walked the short distance to Justice Street. The thought of seeing her sisters put a spring in her step.

Half way down Justice Street, she found number fourteen, a dilapidated building. The window frames were rotting and the green paint on the front door was chipped and dirty. There were several grubby steps leading to the door and everyone was inhabited by men of various ages wearing dirty clothes.

Weaving her way through their slouched bodies, she reached the threshold and pushed the door open to enter.

The sunless and airless hallway reeked. The stale, pungent smell of boiled cabbage and potatoes hung in the air,

A woman beside an open door was berating a tearful child, calling the boy lazy and a good for nothing who hadn't the brains to bring a penny into the family.

When she had run out of complaints, Lizzie asked if she knew which room the Straine family lived.

Scowling, the woman said, "Who wants to know?"

"I'm the elder daughter of Mr and Mrs Straine and I wish to visit my parents and sisters. Do you know which room they occupy?"

The woman started to turn away toward through the open door to her room. "No idea where they are. They left here a fortnight ago. Haven't seen hide or hair of any of them since then. The landlord kicked them out. He was so angry, he lashed out something shocking. Your family ran out into the street with only the clothes on their backs. Not that they had much more than that in the first place."

Lizzie felt anger and bitter disappointment listening to the woman. How could her mother lie so blatantly? Saying they lived here when all the time they did not. What had happened to the girls? Where were they? On the streets?

Disappearing through the open door, the woman slammed it shut.

For several moments, Lizzie remained in the hallway at a loss of what she should do next.

Searching the vicinity seemed the best option. Retracing her steps she went outside and asked the most presentable man in the rabble, if he had any idea where her family had gone? Had anyone seen them since they were thrown out of their room? The answer was surly and not the least bit useful.

Reluctantly, Lizzie went to the back of the row of dilapidated houses and began a search.

The day was coming to a close, when sore footed, she started to walk towards Granny Eliza"s. Lizzie's heart was heavy. Where were her sisters? What had become of them?.

~ ~ ~ ~ ~

Returning home to the old cottage, a fire blazed.

On the table three candles were alight.

An unheard of extravagance.

A cut loaf alongside a half-eaten meat pie, a slab of butter and most surprisingly of all, a shop bought fruit cake were laid out on the small table.

"What's all this Granny Eliza?" Granny Eliza was very bright and cheerful, her face a little pink from the glass or two of rum she had evidently enjoyed during the afternoon.

"I've had a visitor," the old lady grinned.

Putting aside her unhappiness, Lizzie tried to sound cheerful.

"Who?" Lizzie smiled but she was, in truth, surprised. Visitors were as rare as hen's teeth at Granny Eliza's.

"Tom came to visit."

"Oh!" Lizzie was too emotionally drain to ponder what Tom might be doing visiting Granny Eliza with such a big spread. He usually saved such big spreads for Christmas.

Granny Eliza grinned. "Well he turned up this afternoon." Her eyes went to the table. "He brought all this lovely food." She moved quite sprightly over to the old cupboard and took out a bottle of rum with a third of the contents already gone.

"We'll have a glass to celebrate, Lizzie," she said bringing it to the table.

"Celebrate? What are we celebrating?"

Granny Eliza's grin spread. "He came to ask me to move into his house, Lizzie. Isn't it wonderful? I am to be his companion. Oh, Lizzie just think, there will be no more washing and ironing for me. For the first time in my life I will be able to sit and sometimes read. Tom says I'm too old to be working so hard. He said other things too."

Lizzie didn't doubt it.

Granny Eliza had sometimes talked about the romance of her youth, and the way she and Tom looked at each other when he visited each Christmas, she had wondered if the romance would ever be rekindled in their shared old age.

The only thing was Lizzie wasn't ready for that. Not yet.

Lizzie's heart dropped as she looked at the dear old smiling woman. Tears bit at her eyes, Swallowing them, she forced a smile.

"It's wonderful news, Granny Eliza," she said kissing the downy skin of the old lady's cheek. "It really is wonderful news."

Pouring rum into two glasses, Granny Eliza handed one to Lizzie.

"To a better future," the old woman said tipping her glass against Lizzie's.

Lizzie coughed as the fiery liquid hit her throat.

The old lady laughed. "It'll do you good."

Lizzie took another sip but cautiously this time.

"We have talked it through, Lizzie. The rent on this old place is very little. I did the figures and I know you can afford it. If you carry on taking in washing you can afford to stay here. Perhaps get a small girl to help you."

Lizzie went to the old woman and curled up on the floor beside her. Not knowing what to say, she lay her head in Granny Eliza's lap.

"There now Lizzie, you mustn't feel you are being abandoned. I'll only be a few streets away."

Lizzie sniffed the tears back, determined to keep her fear and disappointment to herself.

She glanced around the threadbare room as though seeing it properly for the first time. If she could find her poor sisters she could bring them here and keep them safe.

With the loss of her money to her mother, and without Granny Eliza to manage the business she would have to work very hard to pay the rent next week.

Granny Eliza stroked her hair. "You've been a God send to me, you know Lizzie. And I like to think that God put you in my care too." The old woman stroked Lizzie's hair.

Granny Eliza rose from the corner seat. "I know its sudden Lizzie, but he's coming for me tomorrow."

Lizzie looked into the old woman's face. "Tomorrow?"

"We don't want to wait. Only the good Lord knows how long we've got. You can manage—can't you Lizzie?"

Lizzie smiled through her tears, she longed to pour out her troubles to Granny Eliza, who would give her some wise words, as she had done when Lizzie was a child, but she could not put a blight on Granny Eliza's happiness with her own terrible foolishness.

~ ~ ~ ~

In the early morning light, Lizzie heard the faint sound of the carriage moving off. When she rose, Granny Eliza had left her a note, saying she didn't want to see Lizzie cry again, and reminding her that she wasn't far away.

The day wore on, and Lizzie went through the motions she had done every day since she had lived with Granny Eliza. By afternoon she had placed the irons in trivets over the fire, and ironed the fresh laundry.

In the morning she relit the fire in the chill morning air, and filled the old copper with buckets from the pump and boiled the water and completed the wash, pegged it out, and then made the deliveries of freshly laundered clothes and linens in wrapped brown parcels.

By the next night, silence descended like a dark blanket. Lizzie looked to the fire falling in on itself but decided not to throw on more wood, fearing that she would not be in a position to buy more in the future. Pulling Granny Eliza's chair closer toward the fire, she sat in it for the first time since coming to live with the old lady when she was a perished ten-year old with no home to go to.

Remembering those dark days, tears filled Lizzie's eyes and she began to cry.

The night was long and cold and Lizzie's mind was filled with dreams and memories of her now lost family and the hard years of laundering other people's soiled sheets and clothes. At some point in the night, she woke.

Perhaps she would be like Granny Eliza, a lifetime in this room, working to eat. There would be no happy ending for her as there had been for Granny Eliza.

But nobody in the world deserved happiness more than the kind woman who had taken her in and shown love throughout the years. Lizzie sobbed again until sleep found her once more.

Chapter Ten

On the third day of being alone in the old house, Lizzie finished her chores just as darkness began to fall, and went out of the house to the midden. Returning, she saw a movement near the corner of the old cottage and stopped in her tracks, heart pitter-pattering in her chest.

"Who's there," she said trying to sound unafraid and measuring the distance between the back door of the house and the dark apparition lurking in the shadows.

"Lizzie, it is only me."

Recognising the voice at once, Lizzie scowled.

Her mother came out of the dark shadow of the house. "Where did you get to on Sunday? We waited all day. The girls were very disappointed," she said sounding hard done by.

"What do you mean you waited all day? I came to Justice Street but you had already left. You lied to me. Your old neighbour said that you had gone a fortnight ago. Thrown out by the irate landlord."

"That's a lie, Lizzie. You must have spoken to the mad woman that lives there. One day she will get into so much trouble for her rapscallion ways. She lies all the time, Lizzie. Please take no notice of her."

Lizzie's eyes narrowed in disbelief. "So you are saying you are all still living at number fourteen, Justice Street?"

"Yes, of course. We have nowhere else to go. The last money you so kindly gave us went to pay the landlord, so we didn't lose our home. It is hard to believe how horrible some people can be. Fancy her telling you we had already gone."

Lizzie looked at her mother sceptically, unsure if to believe her or not.

Seeing the uncertain expression on her daughter's face, Sallie Straine's tone became more urgent. "I'm speaking the truth, Lizzie. Come again tomorrow and see your sisters. They are growing so fast you will hardly recognise them."

The thought that her sisters were growing-up and becoming more at risk of being turned out onto the street, convinced Lizzie to see them the next day. She would keep a close eye on her parents and perhaps save the girls from a cruel life of prostitution.

"I'll come in the late afternoon, after work," she said in a monotone.

Her mother smiled. "Oh it will be lovely to have all the family together. Who knows, we may even have a few pennies to buy bread." Her eyes lit. "Even get a peas pudding from Mrs Harrington's new shop. What a treat that would be, Lizzie. A family celebration."

Lizzie was beginning to believe her mother but in the back of her mind she was afraid what was being promised was little more than a fairy tale.

Her eyes went to the house. "I must check on the fire," she said.

"You sound so grown up now Lizzie. Taking care of the old lady are you. She must pay you a pretty penny for your work."

Lizzie kept the news that Granny Eliza had moved out, to herself.

"I don't get much money," she said. "I'm glad to be fed and have a roof over my head. The old lady has been very kind to me."

Her mother tutted. "Still nice to have a warm place to lay your head, Lizzie. My girls will not get that tonight. There's no money to spare for a bit of coal or food. The girls will go hungry tonight."

Lizzie frowned. "Is father not working at all?"

Mrs Straine sniffed loudly. "I told you last time I saw you that your father is ill and unable to do a day's work. There's no money in the house, Lizzie."

Lizzie sighed inwardly.

Mrs Straine caught hold of Lizzie's sleeve. "If you could give me enough for some food for tonight and some for tomorrow's rent, the girls will be safe from your father's threats of putting them out. Please help us, Lizzie. I dread to see my girls on the streets with dirty rascals touching them."

"I don't have much, Mother."

"Just give me what you can. The girls will be so grateful. They will not go to bed hungry tonight if you help us."

"Wait here," Lizzie said coldly.

Turning back into the house, she went to the cupboard and took out the jar of coins. Taking a few, holding them in her hand, she went back outside.

"This is all I can spare," she said handing the money to her mother who took it eagerly.

It passed through Lizzie's mind that she may not have enough money to buy soap for this week's washing.

"We will see you tomorrow Lizzie," her mother said suddenly in a hurry to leave the old yard.

Watching her retreat, Lizzie sighed.

Dejected she went back into the house and closed the door. Going to the fire, she threw a log onto the dying embers. It would be a miracle if the girls benefitted from the money, it was much more likely to go into a barman's pocket to pay for gin. As she sat in Granny Eliza's chair she allowed the orange glow from the coals to mesmerise her and a loose plan began to form in her mind.

If the girls come to live here, and take a share of the work, perhaps we can get by. And the girls will be safe here, there won't be any need to keep parting with money to my mother.

As soon as she could tomorrow, she would talk to her sisters and there would be a solution. It would work, she would make it so.

With that settling thought, she closed her eyes and fell asleep almost instantly.

Hardly stirring all night, she woke to weak sunshine glinting through the gap in the small threadbare curtain. Throwing back the grey blanket and thin cotton sheet, she put a log on the few embers still glowing at the bottom of the hearth and put the kettle ready for when the wood flamed.

Though she was poorer by several coins, she felt cheerful. The idea of her sisters coming to live with her gladdened her heart. Her sisters would be happier and more secure and content to help with the laundry. With hard work they would manage to survive reasonably well, although they may need to take in more washing. And Lizzie would not be living a solitary life. The three of them would be together.

The log caught, sending smoke and sparks up the blackened chimney. Putting the kettle to the flame, she threw a shawl over her cotton shift, slipped her bare feet into her boots, and went out of the kitchen and down to the midden.

When she returned, she had everything in her mind mapped out. The girls could sleep in Granny Eliza's old bed in the attic and she would remain on the straw mattress beside the fire. Tonight she would bring them home with her.

She would make a stew of vegetables and buy a loaf of bread, there was no time to bake today, she had washing and ironing to do before she went to Justice Street. Later, after they had eaten their fill, they would sit around the fire and talk until they were all too tired to share another thought.

The day passed reasonably quickly, helped by the fact she was happy to be making plans..

When she got paid for this week's laundry, she hoped to have enough money to buy essentials for the girls.

At four o'clock she banked up the fire as she wanted the room cosy for when the girls arrived. The bread oven was hot enough for her to place the pot of vegetables. This done she took a coin from her cherished small hoard to buy bread, threw her knitted shawl around her shoulders and went out.

Locking up the house, she put the key in her skirt pocket and set off, her heart light at the prospect of being with her siblings once more. If she could have one wish in the world it would be to save them from the harsh exploitation of their parents.

It took almost twenty minutes to reach Justice Street. She walked along the cobbled roads, her eyes on the dirty tenement houses and the people sitting on the steps. Lizzie was glad to be out of the tenements, she was happy her sisters were leaving the neighbourhood this afternoon.

A few children were playing in the street close to number fourteen and she looked for her sisters but they were not with the small group.

Reaching the house, she trotted up the front steps and went through the dirty chipped door into the hallway. The house was noisy, every room holding an entire family within. Climbing the stairs she went along the narrow hallway, listening intently for the familiar sound of her family.

Behind every closed door there was the noise of raised voices, babies crying, mothers shouting for peace. Emanating from every tiny home there was the smell of boiled cabbage.

Climbing to the next floor, she went along the narrow corridor and hearing similar sounds, she knocked on the last door.

A woman in a black dress, her hair wild as though she had just risen from her bed, looked at her suspiciously.

"I'm sorry to disturb you," Lizzie said. "But I am looking for my family, Mr and Mrs Straine and their young daughters."

"You are wasting your time. They left here at the beginning of the month. Landlord kicked them out with only what they had on their backs."

"But that can't be so. I saw my mother only yesterday. She said they were still living here," Lizzie said, panic rising.

The woman gave a sharp burst of laughter. "And you believed the gin soaked drunk. The woman isn't sober a moment of the day. You are best off without them."

With that she closed the door. Lizzie was rooted to the ground, her plans and hopes falling like autumn leaves around her.

She was tempted to knock the door again and ask the woman if she was sure. In her heart she knew it was a waste of time. Her family had gone. She had been duped again by her mother. Where were her sisters?

Already out on the streets selling themselves to keep their parents in gin? Oh she hoped not. Surely even her mother and father would not sink to such a dreadful low.

Turning away, her heart in her boots, she went along the hallway and down the stairs.

Just before she reached the front door, she knocked on the last door. The woman she had seen previously opened it. She looked displeased to be disturbed.

"Good day," Lizzie said. "I'm still looking for the Straine family. Do you have any idea where they may be?"

"No. I don't. Though someone said they saw the girls last week. You probably don't want to know where they were and what they were doing."

"Oh, but I do. They are my poor sisters. It is really important that I find them."

"Take a look on Ardwick Street. They were seen on the pavement there. Though they have probably moved on by now."

Lizzie turned away. Going outside, passing by the men smoking their pipes on the steps, she reached the pavement. There was no spring in her step as she went towards Ardwick Street, a dirty place known for harbouring thieves, prostitutes and exotic people running opium dens.

It took her an hour to reach the place and she wandered up and down hoping to see a face she knew. Several men accosted her and it didn't take too long before she was running from the place, too afraid to remain a moment longer.

Footsore when she reached home, she let herself into the cottage. The fire had gone out and the vegetables were dried up in the pot.

Sinking onto Granny Eliza's chair, she buried her face in her hands and wept with disappointment and fear for her poor sisters. She was too late, they were lost to her.

Eventually the chill of the room moved her to rise, and she threw kindling onto the fire and relit the wood. With a little water and a stir the stew could be revived to being edible. For all her woe she was hungry as she hadn't eaten a morsel since her early breakfast of bread and dripping.

With the stew looking slightly better, she poured it into a dish and sat with it on her lap eating it with a spoon. Her thoughts went to Granny Eliza, and she wondered what she was doing now, most probably enjoying a delicious dinner at a proper table with Tom.

Lizzie found it impossible not to feel a little happier thinking about Granny Eliza's new happiness, yet a tear slid down her cheek. Brushing it away, another tear fell. She buried her face in her hands again and sobbed, the feeling of aloneness overwhelming her. As she cried, she came to a decision.

Tomorrow, she would seek out Adam and ask his advice. She would tell him all that had happened. She did not believe he would abandon her. Instead he would advise her the best course of action. With luck and Adam's help, she would find her sisters if they were in the vicinity of Ardwick Street.

~ ~ ~ ~ ~

Lizzie had laundered and hung the next day's washing and delivered the last of the laundry to her customers.

She thought to go to Adams place of work at the warehouse on Fenchurch Street and find him, but slipping in and out of the huge expanse of buildings was not an option.

She wouldn't know where to begin to find him, if she were caught inside, she might well be accused of thieving.

No, Lizzie decided, she couldn't risk being accused of anything at all. Instead, she set off to Albert Street. She would catch him on the way home, and talk with him then.

Grabbing a load of un-ironed laundry she folded it into her basket, so any-one seeing her would simply assume she was going about her business, and avoid any unnecessary conversations.

As the day began to close in, she saw him walking up Albert Street. Half sobbing she ran toward him, the laundry bag hoisted on her hip. "Adam," she called to him.

"Lizzie, what is wrong," he said sounding worried.

Tears fell from Lizzie's eyes. "Oh Adam, I had to come and see you. I am so very worried.."

"I have been looking for my sisters but cannot find them. I hoped you may be able help me."

Adam's eyes were full of questions.

Lizzie had only ever told Adam that Granny Eliza was her own grandmother, and she was sent to live with Granny Eliza as Granny had needed the help. If Adam had asked any questions about her family, she been vague and quickly changed topic.

It was a small deceit but it had saved Lizzy a lot of explanation, and if Adam had doubted her, he never let on. In the early days of their friendship she had seen a flash of compassion in his eyes.

He had soon stayed away from the topic of her family altogether.

"Of course I will." He looked down at the package in his hands. "I have to deliver this to mam. As soon as I have done that, I will come to your house. We can talk there."

"Won't she ask why you're leaving again?"

"I'll tell her I've got an errand for Uncle, then she won't ask any questions."

Gratitude welled in her heart. "Thank you, Adam. You are the best friend I could wish for." She gave a worried, watery smile.

"Don't worry, Lizzie. I'll be there very shortly, I promise," he said returning her half smile.

Turning away, Lizzie retraced her steps and entered the house, where she sat huddled at the table, waiting. As the dusk cast its shadows through the tiny windows, she became lost in her thoughts and barely noticed the darkness. Before she knew it, she heard a light knocking on the door.

The door to the latch lifted and Adam put his head in. Are you there, Lizzie?

"Yes, Adam."

"Why are you sitting in the dark?" Where is Granny Eliza?

"Oh, it is dark isn't it! I'll light a candle."

He put his hand on her shoulder gently. "You stay there. I'll light the candle." His eyes went to the dead fire. "I'll light that too. It is cold in here."

As Adam lit the candle, he caught her eyes and was disturbed by the unhappiness he saw there.

He worked without effort and once the fire was flaming he came to the table and sat beside her. "Now tell me what has happened."

"Adam, whatever I tell you, you please say you won't hate me for it?"

"Lizzie! Of course I won't hate you for anything. We're friends you and I – aren't we?" Lizzie nodded and wiped her eyes with the back of her hand.

"Adam, Granny Eliza is not my granny. She found me in her courtyard, when I was only nine or ten years old. I was frightened and lost because my parents had done me a terrible deed. They sent me on an errand, and when I got back to the room, they had packed up and left with my sisters and I was all alone."

Adam's face clouded in sorrow as he listened to Lizzie's tale. "The things I told you, about having my mother and father sending me to live with my granny to give her a helping hand, it was not true. I lied to you. I was so very embarrassed and your family seems so nice, even well off, and I just….." Her words trailed off but her eyes were pleading with him to understand.

"It's alright, Lizzie please don't worry. I always suspected something was not quite right with your story. You never talked about your mam or your pa, or even your sisters." Lizzie sniffed her tears back and gazed into the fire, not daring to look at him. "It really is alright, but Lizzie, where *is* Granny Eliza?" His voice had once more grown worried.

"Well, you see, That's the other thing that has happened. Granny Eliza has a friend Tom, she's had him for a long time, and well, he finally asked her to be his companion and he would take care of her. And she—" A sob broke through her words, "and she left. And I told her it was alright and it's not like I won't see her anymore, but oh Adam, I am all alone, I am so alone now."

"But you'll be able to manage won't you? You've been doing most everything for a while now, from all I know."

"But That's the other thing." Lizzie stopped and swallowed a sob. "It's my mother, she's been coming here. She found me and—and she wanted money." Lizzie looked at him wide eyed, not daring to tell him how very foolish she had been.

It was one thing to admit her shame of the lie, but to tell him she gave almost every penny she had to someone who had abandoned her with nothing—it was the same reason she couldn't have told Granny Eliza, he would scorn her for a fool.

Adam's brows turned inwards, "Lizzie, did she want you to come home? Maybe there was a good reason...." He looked at her helplessly realising the futility of his argument.

"There was a reason," Lizzie said bitterly. "She told me she needed money for rent, to keep my sisters safe.. She told me if I gave her the money my father wouldn't put my sisters out to work on the streets.

She said I could see them, but when I went to the address she gave me, the tenants told me they were thrown out a fortnight ago. And then the lady told me my sister was working on Ardwick Street."

"It's not all bad Lizzie" Adam said gently. "You can continue with the laundry and if you find your sisters, you can bring them here, give them a job, give them a home. They'll be safe here with you. And with the three of you, you will earn enough. Maybe even save a little bit."

The tiny room had begun to lose the chill on the air, and in the glow of the firelight and the candle, she felt a modicum of hope. All that Adam had said, made sense. Indeed, hadn't she thought those very same things herself?

~ ~ ~ ~ ~

Lizzie went over his words again as she made up her bed beside the fire and eventually climbed in and pulled the grey blanket up to her chin. She lay for a while thinking back to when the girls were small and what it must be like now.

She longed to find them and to make their future better. Talking with Adam had calmed her mind and she began again to plan ahead to a time when her sisters would be sharing the cottage with her.

Relighting the fire and dressing in the warmth of the first fiery flames, the kettle gently steamed, ready for her first cup of tea of the morning. She made a mental list of the customers she must visit, to collect their dirty washing. With luck she could return sheets and other things tomorrow, she would pay the rent, and secure what she would need for the laundry and then she would find her sisters.

Letting herself out of the house and locking the door, she set off towards Trafalgar Street to her first customer.

It was almost midday when Lizzie returned home. Letting herself into the house, she dumped a pile of washing she had carried for the last half-hour onto the floor.

Rebuilding the fire and refilling the cauldrons, she set to work on the day's washing.

Though the house was quiet without Granny Eliza's chatter, Lizzie turned her mind to how happy the old lady would be with Tom beside her.

By mid-afternoon there was enough breeze to hang out the washing and before the sun began to drift towards the horizon, Lizzie brought the damp sheets in and draped the linen over the overhead drying rack to air.

There was a drop of sack in the bottle that Tom had brought for Granny Eliza. Lizzie went to the cupboard and took a water tumbler, and the bottle, and sat beside the fire to enjoy a tipple of sweet sherry.

She had no sooner put the glass to her lips, when the cottage door flew open and her parents stepped over the threshold in a rush. Her father, with a grin from ear to ear, closed the door with a bang.

"Oh, so it's true," her mother exclaimed loudly.

Putting the glass aside on the floor, Lizzie jumped out of her chair. "What are you doing here?"

"We have come to visit our daughter," her mother said innocently.

Lizzie was angry. "Perhaps to explain why you lied to me about still living in Justice Street," she yelled.

"Lizzie don't take on so. You know the difficulties we have."

"Difficulties you do not spare my sisters enduring."

"The girls are fine. They have taken up with gentlemen sponsors who will take care of them." Walking across the room, her mother sat in the chair Lizzie had just vacated. "That is why we are moving in with you—now that they're off on their own. Since the old lady has left, you'll be in need of company."

Lizzie was speechless and she stared open mouthed as her father went to the cupboard and took the cut loaf of bread and piece of cheese out.

"We will be no trouble to you, Lizzie," he said coming to the table with a small smile on his mouth.

Her mother pointed to the washing on the drying rack. "We don't expect you to carry on taking in washing, Lizzie. I couldn't bear having other people's dirty clothes around me."

Hands on her hips, Lizzie stared at her mother. "And what do you expect me to do instead?" She knew the answer before her mother even looked up from the glass she had taken off the floor and put to her wet lips.

"The girls have managed, there's no reason you shouldn't join them on Ardwick Street. It'll pay more than this carry-on." She pointed to the drying racks.

"Who told you Granny Eliza had left here?" Lizzie said in a hostile tone.

"Someone in a local public house. What does it matter? We need somewhere to stay and you have room for us."

Sallie Straine sniffed loudly. "After all, we are your parents. Blood is thicker than water."

Lizzie gave a phony laugh. "Pity you didn't think of that when you abandoned me at ten-years old."

Her mother shrugged and took a mouthful of sack from the glass. "You managed," she said indifferently.

Lizzie's father went back to the cupboard and rummaged amongst the contents. Finding Lizzie's money jar, he brought it out and rattled it.

"So you have savings," he said. "Why didn't you offer your mother this?"

Tears of frustration welled in Lizzie's eyes. "Give that back to me."

He rattled it again. "Finders keepers." He laughed.

Lizzie knew it was useless to fight with him. He would clout her, and hard, if he didn't get his way.

Grabbing her coat off the nail on the back of the door, Lizzie threw it over her green shawl. Opening the door onto the raw night, she ran out.

Running, she fled down the street, not considering what she might do, where she might go.

She passed shop doorways where men and boys were sheltering from the cold night, it went through her mind that unless she went back and confronted her parents, she was homeless too.

An empty bottle was in her path and instead of avoiding it, she kicked it hard with the toe of her boot.

It went flying down the street and then smashed to smithereens on the cobbles. The sound was mildly satisfying. As her emotional energy ebbed out, she leaned against a wall, a stitch jabbing at her side, breathing hard, she massaged the stitch until it abated.

She thought of going to Granny Eliza, but she knew, she would not do that. She would not disturb Granny Eliza's new-found happiness, and mar it with the despicable news of her parents invading the home that Granny Eliza had made for many years past.

It would be too much for Granny Eliza to know that Lizzie had lost the cottage, and all of her money too.

She kept walking until she found herself outside the warehouse where Adam worked.

Not knowing what to do, or where to go, Lizzie walked slowly past the vast buildings. If she could find a place to sleep safely for the night, she would wait for Adam. It was all that Lizzie could think to do.

Knowing that there existed an alley that would lead to the docking area for loading and unloading, Lizzie counted the number of buildings along from the beginning of the row of warehouses to the warehouse where Adam worked, finding her way to the lane that ran behind the building. Moving quickly, she slipped to the side of the stables.

Did she dare to go in? Would she be discovered if she slept too deeply? The thought of the heat of the horses and a bed of hay tempted her. Climbing over the short gate, she dropped down quietly. Horses nickered as she moved.

Finding her way to the ladder that led to the hay loft, Lizzie carefully climbed the steps taking care to make no sound. Finding the furthest corner, away from where the grooms lodgings were, she curled into a ball.

As her mind calmed, she thought what to do. She would wake before the groom, but if she didn't she would hear the horses would nicker and whinny and she would lay quietly until she could sneak away.

Feeling secure in her plan, and too tired and worn to care much more, Lizzie fell to a sound sleep. When the morning sun streaked its grey light in through the cracks of walls of the old building, Lizzie woke instantly. Slipping out of the stables, she hurried to the streets where the business of the day was already beginning to stir.

~ ~ ~ ~ ~

Lizzie waited watchfully for Adam. The moment she spied him walking down Fenchurch Street she waited until he was near to the warehouse. "Adam, Adam, wait."

At the sound of his name, Adam turned his head toward the voice. Shock fell over his face seeing the dishevelled Lizzie standing before him. "Lizzie! Whatever has happened?"

Taking her by the arm he led her away from the entrance, away from the throngs of workers moving into the various floors of the warehouse.

"Lizzie," he whispered. "Whatever is wrong?"

Still guiding her away, he led her to a café.

As they waited for the café owner to unlock the door, she began to tell him that had been forced from her home and she had spent the night in the stables not knowing where else to go.

She was shivering with cold by the time the café opened, and Adam led her to a seat closest to the warm oven. Ordering a pot of tea, eggs, bacon and toast. He listened silently, his expression changed from concern to anger as the story unfolded. When she had finished, Lizzie sipped at her tea.

"Come Lizzie – eat up." He watched her push the food around her plate. "There'll be a solution, we'll think of one."

Eventually he said, "You can't go back there, Lizzie. Your father sounds an absolute scoundrel and a violent one at that."

Lizzie nodded her agreement.

"There is a solution. My uncle is looking for a kitchen maid. I will tell him tonight that you are perfect for the job."

"Adam, would you do that for me?"

"Of course. You *are* perfect for the job. There's no doubt about it."

She looked up into his face. "Where would I stay tonight Adam?" she asked timidly. Should I sneak into the stable?"

A frown crossed over his brow. "No. it's too much of a risk. Better that you stay in a room."

"Oh Adam, I can't do that — I have no way to pay."

"We are friends Lizzie and I will pay for your lodgings until you can go to my uncle's house."

Lizzie held her tears back.

"Thank you Adam. I'll pay you back, as soon as I've got my first wage."

Adam smiled at her. "It will work out Lizzie, I'm sure it will, but I must go, if I am to see my uncle. Will you at least finish your breakfast? Pressing some coins into her hand, he said "Meet me back here at noon, and we will find you safe lodgings."

He was gone in an instant and Lizzie was left alone in the café.

~ ~ ~ ~ ~

Lizzie was back at the café at precisely noon. Scanning the street she saw Adam exit by the front of the warehouse and waved to him.

"I have good news," he said cheerfully as he reached her. "My uncle says you can go to his house today and start work as a kitchen maid, he's already sent word to my aunt that you are coming."

Lizzie should have been happy, but instead she cried.

"Come on Lizzie, it will all be all right. Buck-up."

"I am grateful Adam, I truly am." Lizzie brushed her tears aside, with a silent apology to Granny Eliza for losing her little cottage.

~ ~ ~ ~ ~

It was almost midday when she stood outside the Lynch household.

Lizzie had shaken out her coat well, and painstakingly removed any bit of dirt or hay from her hair, and smoothed out everything as best she could.

Going around to the back of the house, following the sign for tradesmen, she came to the back door. Tugging the brass bell-pull she stood back waiting for the door to open.

Though her feet were tired and she was hungry and thirsty, Lizzie forced a smile.

The door opened and a woman wearing a black dress stood on the threshold.

Lizzie, looking up, said, "I'm Lizzie Straine. I have been employed as a kitchen maid by Mr Lynch."

The woman many years older than Lizzie, sniffed. "You had better come in. Is Mrs Lynch expecting you?"

"I hope so," Lizzie said suddenly alarmed that she may not be expected.

Following the woman into the house, and passing through a small vestibule and into the kitchen, Lizzie looked carefully to the shining brass, clean range and copper-bottomed pans hanging from a row of hooks on the wall. She didn't doubt it would be her job to scour and polish the copper and brass and black the range regularly.

"I will go and find Mrs Lynch and tell her you are here," the woman said, disappearing through the kitchen door.

Lizzie had a moment to further inspect the kitchen as she waited, her eyes going to the dark oak dresser and the blue and white crockery arranged upon it. There seemed to be a pot and a plate for every eventuality.

However was she to remember what went with what? Her original home had no crockery beside two plates and one dish for collecting peas pudding in.

Granny Eliza's home had a little more than that, with four plates, two mugs, and posh cups and saucers for visitors, but here there appeared to be dozens and dozens of every shape and size imaginable.

Her thoughts were interrupted as the kitchen door opened and the woman returned. Her face was dour.

"The master of the house told Mrs Lynch to expect you," she snapped.

Lizzie sighed in relief. At least she didn't have to explain herself and wait while it was determined if she should stay or go.

"I will escort you to Mrs Lynch's private sitting room. Follow me, Straine."

Matching the woman's steps, Lizzie went out of the kitchen along the wide and lengthy corridor to the front of the house.

Knocking lightly on the door, she went in. "Sorry to disturb you, Mrs Lynch. I have the new maid here for your inspection."

Turning, she beckoned Lizzie to enter.

There was no expression of welcome or friendliness on Mrs Lynch's face as she looked at Lizzie.

"Do exactly as Mrs Halbard tells you. Do not be lazy. I do not expect you to have followers or mix with anyone of the lower orders. Do you understand?" She looked fiercely at Lizzie.

Feeling like a mouse before a cat, Lizzie nodded quickly.

"Mrs Halbard, take her upstairs and see she gets into a uniform."

Her nose turned up slightly as she looked to Lizzie's old coat and the green shawl showing at the opening.

"Yes, Mrs Lynch. At once." Opening the door with a key hanging on her chatelaine chain, Mrs Halbard said, "This will be your room. I expect you to keep it spotless. I will do random checks to make sure everything is kept in order. Do you understand?"

Lizzie nodded. "Yes, Mrs Halbard."

"Good. Now change into the uniform on the bed and come down to the kitchen immediately. There's work to be done. You can begin by checking the fires in the downstairs rooms."

Lizzie stood in the middle of the small room, listening to the woman's footsteps retreating. When silence fell, she went to the bed and sat on the edge of the thin mattress. She was fifteen-years old and this was the first proper bed she would sleep in.

Eyeing the grey uniform on the bed, she knew it was going to be far too big for her. Following orders, she slipped out of the coat she was wearing, untied her green shawl, unbuttoned her frock and stood in her shift for a moment. Taking up the grey dress she slipped it on and placed the white cap over her hair and made her way as quickly as she could, back down the stairs to the kitchen.

Chapter Eleven

May 1880

Life in the Lynch household proved to be hard and monotonous. Many times, she wished she was back in her house with Granny Eliza. The work had been hard, but there had been a great loss of freedom she had only now begun to understand.

Rising before five o'clock in the morning, she began her day cleaning out the black range in the kitchen and relighting the fire. It was always a relief when the fire caught as it was important it was going well, so cook could be ready to prepare early breakfast for Mr Lynch.

With the range fire burning, Lizzie raked out and cleaned the fireplaces and lit the fires to warm the rooms before the family descended the stairs.

Before seven o'clock Lizzie took a bucket of water and scrubbing brush to clean the front step, polishing the brass plaque on the wall with the number of the house upon it.

Indoors again Lizzie turned her attention to the dishes in the kitchen waiting to be washed and dried and put away on the dresser.

The moment Mr Lynch appeared for his breakfast, Lizzie dashed up the stairs and took the used chamber-pot from his chamber and emptied and cleaned it before returning it to its rightful place. The next chore was to empty the slops in the washing bowl, clean the dresser and refill the cold water jug for use later.

Back downstairs she washed the dishes and pots and pans cook had used. Carried out slops and brought in fresh water from the well in the backyard beyond the kitchen.

The moment Mrs Lynch appeared for her breakfast, Lizzie would wait until she was seated and then dash up the back stairs and make her way to Mrs Lynch's bedchamber. With the washing slops and the chamber pot emptied she cleaned the dresser and filled the water jug. The housemaid would clean and tidy the bed chamber whilst Lizzie went back down to begin her day's chores of polishing and cleaning in the kitchen.

The routine hardly ever changed and although Lizzie longed for a day off, she waited until the first month had passed by before she was granted an afternoon to herself.

Adam came to visit his aunt and uncle weekly and there were occasions when she managed to speak to him for a few minutes in the kitchen yard.

Mrs Halbard proved to be a hard taskmaster. Lizzie worked from five o'clock in the morning until all chores were over. Once the family had finished their evening meal she would wash and dry the dishes and clean the kitchen before retiring.

Too exhausted to do anything but sleep, and fed only what was left after the family and upper staff had eaten their meal, Lizzie lost weight and her uniform hung further off her bony frame.

Scolded and slapped for looking untidy, Mrs Halbard demanded she alter the dress until it fitted her properly. Sewing by the light of a solitary candle, Lizzie worked late for several nights to make the dress fit.

Coming into the kitchen one morning, Lizzie found cook already making pastry. For a moment she thought she must be dreadfully late.

"There you are, Straine," Cook said unusually cheerfully. "As soon as you have completed the morning chores, I want you to help the housemaid to make up young Mr Lynch's bed chamber. He will be arriving this evening. Also his cousin, Mr Treadwell will be visiting for dinner tonight."

The news that Adam would be in the house later, cheered Lizzie, and her chores seemed less laborious than usual. If there was any luck to be had, there might be a chance that she would be able to slip out and speak with him when he took his pipe into the garden to smoke.

The day raced by and as darkness fell. Lizzie listened for the sound of a carriage pulling up outside the house. She was crossing the hallway, carefully carrying a vase of flowers into the dining room, when the sound of the brass knocker, echoed through the Foyer.

"Come-on Lizzie, don't take all day about it Jones the footman admonished as he pushed past her and went to the front door. The door was barely opened, before it flew wide and Adam and Mr Joshua Lynch burst through the entrance.

It was obvious that Mr Lynch had enjoyed a tipple or two at a tavern. "There you are, Fannie," he said cheerfully to Lizzie.

Adam smiled. "This is Lizzie, not Fannie." He looked briefly into Lizzie's eyes.

"Fannie, Lizzie, all the girls look delicious to me after so many months at sea," Joshua guffawed.

Mrs Lynch came through the drawing room door. Opening her arms wide she went quickly to greet her elder son. "Joshua darling, how wonderful to see you."

"Mother dear," he said. "You are as beautiful as ever."

She slapped his chest playfully. "You are a lovable scoundrel, Joshua."

"I always tell my cousins, you stopped at one son because you were extremely pleased with the result." he said planting a kiss on her powdery cheek.

"Joshua, you are incorrigible," she said returning the kiss.

Without looking in the family's direction, Lizzie came out of the dining room and crossed the hallway silently.

"A new maid, mother. What has become of Fanny?"

"She found a man to take care of her and married him last week."

He pretended to look crestfallen. "I should have arrived ten days ago. I swear little Fanny would have forgotten her beau if I had been on the scene."

Mrs Lynch slapped his arm. "Behave, Joshua. Especially in front of the servants. Now come into the drawing room, your father is waiting to greet you. He has already poured glasses of sack."

Dinner was an elaborate affair that Lizzie as a kitchen maid was excluded from serving at table. She caught a trace of the jollity at the dining table, as the door was opened for the house maid to carry in dishes.

It was hard not to be envious of Adam, enjoying himself so very much—well fed, wine at his elbow, the good company of his cousin telling him amusing tales of the sea. It made Lizzie feel mean to think this way. Adam was her friend, and he had always been good to her.

When dinner was over and the family had retired to their bedchambers, Cook sat in a fireside chair with her feet up on the fender around the range. At the far side of the kitchen, Lizzie was still washing pots at the long narrow sink, there had been no opportunity to see Adam.

Glancing at Lizzie, Cook said, "Go into the dining room and check that the table is cleared properly. Bring the linen tablecloth to me ready for the laundry tomorrow."

Lizzie dried her hands on a small towel and then went to the kitchen door and crossed the hall.

An oil lamp was still burning on a console table. For a moment she considered carrying the lamp into the dining room.

Deciding the light would stretch beyond the hall, she left the lamp where it was and went in. The room was warm, the aroma of the evening lingered in the still air and the embers of the fire gave a red glow in the marble fireplace.

Suddenly she realised she was not alone. For a brief moment she thought Adam had stayed behind to talk to her.

The moment a voice said, "Lizzie." She knew immediately it was Joshua Lynch standing in the darkness and her heart jumped.

"I'm so sorry," she said. "I didn't know anyone was in here. I came to get the tablecloth."

He scooped the cloth off the table and placed it in her hands, his fingertips touching the delicate flesh of her inner arms. His voice was warm and friendly. "Good night, Lizzie," he said. "Sleep well. No doubt you have worked hard so we could enjoy ourselves. Thank you."

He past her so closely, she felt the warmth of his body.

Chapter Twelve

Another week passed by without seeing Adam.

Several times Mr Joshua came into the kitchen to see cook and steal one of her delicious pastries or a small cake. Every time their paths crossed, Lizzie was aware he was looking closely at her, a friendly expression in his eyes.

She was fascinated by the tales Cook told of Mr Joshua's adventures. Cook had known Joshua all of his life and she followed his sailing voyages as closely as the Lynch family allowed.

Monday morning dawned, and rising before everyone else in the household, Lizzie lit the range in the kitchen. Once it was burning fiercely she went to rake out the dead fires and relight the fires in the rooms that the family would occupy early in the day.

Coming into the breakfast room to attend the dormant fire there, Lizzie noticed that only two places were set at the dining table for breakfast.

The task of laying the table was usually done by the housekeeper the night before. Lizzie assumed that Mrs Lynch was breakfasting in her bedchamber.

Kneeling at the hearth, raking out the ashes, Lizzie thought of the banter which usually passed between father and son when they were at the table.

Mr Lynch junior's laughter ringing out over Mr Lynch senior's, more sedate chortle. She only caught the family jollity if she was passing through the hall on an errand for Mrs Halbard, but it was pleasant to hear the convivial tones.

It often reminded her of the life she had enjoyed with Granny Eliza. The old lady had loved to chuckle at memories of Lizzie's early life with her and the things she had said as a small child.

She had especially liked to recall Lizzie's comment to the butcher of a *'fat goose and not a scrawny one like he had sent the previous Christmas.'*

With the fire gently burning in the grate, Lizzie stood, shaking ash off her beige cotton apron. Glancing at the tall clock ticking in the corner of the room, she hurried to make the preparations to scrub the front door step before the family rose from their warm beds.

Walking quickly to the kitchen, she went out through the back door to the yard beyond and drew icy cold water from the well there.

Carrying the slopping bucket around the back of the house, she came through the small gate used by the tradesmen, and made her way to the front step.

Kneeling on the cold and damp mosaic path, she skimmed the bristles of a scrubbing bush across the water and then began to clean the step, removing marks made by the passage of boots and shoes on the pale yellow stone.

Pulling a duster from her apron pocket, she gave a quick flip over the brass number plate. Then lifting the bucket, she emptied the contents on the pavement where it made a small river across the flagstones beyond the black iron railings.

The chore finished, she went cheerfully towards the back of the house and the door leading to the kitchen, looking forward to hearing the deep tones of Mr Lynch's voice and the cheery tone of Joshua Lynch's conversation in the breakfast room.

Coming into the house, she was met by silence. Cook wasn't yet in the kitchen. There was no sign of Mrs Halbard. Mystifyingly there was a serious lack of aroma of frying mutton and bacon.

Walking across the kitchen flagstones, she opened the door into the hallway and listened but there was no sound coming from the breakfast room.

Closing the door she came to the range and put a full kettle to heat on the hob. A few minutes later, Cook came into the warm room. Her face was blank, without a trace of the smile that had been there throughout Mr Joshua's stay.

Though terrified of arousing the wrath of the cook, Lizzie asked softly, "Is something wrong, Cook?"

Cook tut-tutted. "No. Just have to get back to the mundane again."

"Mundane?" Lizzie asked, not understanding.

Cook's voice was sharp, "Yes, the mundane. Now Mr Joshua has left for a sea voyage there will be little laughter in this house."

"Has he gone?" Lizzie asked with a slight surprise in her voice.

Cook slapped a skillet down. "Yes, he's gone."

"Where's he gone to?" Lizzie asked, curious as to Cook's ill mood.

"Lord knows. Over the sea and far away. Don't expect he will return for many a month, if not longer."

"Oh!"

"Don't stand there looking like someone simple-minded. Get a move on. There's plenty to do," the woman said bad-temperedly.

"Yes, Cook." The house would be droll without Mr Joshua to gladden the hearts of Cook and Mr and Mrs Lynch.

Lizzie went to the breakfast room to check on the fire there. Coming into the room her eyes went to the empty place at the table. It had been a good change to have Mr Joshua's laughter about the house.

Now she had to get used to the everyday again. Long working hours, poor food, and absolutely nothing to smile about unless Adam paid a visit and they might find a moment together.

The day was long and Lizzie was pleased when eventually Mrs Lynch sent orders to the kitchen for an early dinner to be served in the dining room.

An hour before the designated time, Lizzie built up the fire, swept the hearth, and checked that everything was in order in the room. Removing a fallen petal from the flowers on the table, her eyes lingered on the vacant place where Mr Joshua's cutlery had been set for the past weeks.

With a sigh, she left the room and went back to the kitchen to wash pots.

Long days went by with no sight of Adam. Lizzie was beginning to worry he may have caught the influenza that was rife at that time in London and the suburbs.

By chance, as she was coming out of the withdrawing room with a feather duster in her hand she almost bumped into the senior Mr Lynch.

"Good morning, Sir," she said softly.

He gave a sharp nod of his head but said nothing.

Lizzie tried her utmost to pluck up the courage to ask about Adam but Mr Lynch passed into the room and closed the door behind him. Standing quite still, her bottom lip caught between her teeth, she took a step closer and was just about to knock and enter, when Mr Lynch came out again. She feared terribly that he may think she had been eavesdropping.

"Straine," he said sharply. "You can save me the bother of informing Cook that we will be four for dinner tonight. Mrs Lynch will be down shortly to advise what is required."

It was on the tip of Lizzie's tongue to ask if Mr Treadwell would be one of the guests but a piercing stare from Mr Lynch made her move quickly to the kitchen to seek Cook.

The entire day Lizzie hoped that Adam was not ill with influenza and, that he would appear later. Maybe, they would find a few moments to exchange news in the back garden, when Adam went out to smoke after dinner.

Darkness descended at six o'clock. Lizzie went around the house lighting extra lamps, aware that at any moment the expected guests would arrive. Then, the question of whether Adam was a guest would be answered.

She was lighting the two oil lamps on the landing when she heard Adam's cheerful voice in the downstairs hall. A rush of relief charged through her and it was almost impossible not to gasp with delight. She leaned a little over the landing balustrade to get a glimpse of him. Just at that moment

Adam looked up and caught her eye and he sent a warm smile to her. Lizzie was surprised just how pleased she was to see him and doubly pleased he had smiled so sweetly to her.

She watched Jones take Adam's coat, and usher him into the withdrawing room.

The brass door knocker sounded again. Lizzie was curious as to whom the fourth guest might be, and busied herself dusting the newels.

Jones appeared from the small cloakroom and moved quickly to answer the door, but not before turning to glare at her. Afraid she would earn a clip around the ear for dawdling, Lizzie came down the stairs quickly and disappeared into the kitchen.

Cook had boiled a suet pudding, it had been steaming the entire afternoon in a pan at the back of the hob.

As the back door had been kept firmly shut against the cold day the steam had lingered, and rivulets of water trickled down to the copper pans that hung on a stretcher below the ceiling. Lizzie knew that come tomorrow she would have the job of shining the pans anew.

Neither cook nor Mrs Halbard were in a good mood but it hardly mattered to Lizzie. She was just happy to know that Adam was well, and he was here in the same house as she was, and there was a chance that they may get to spend a few moments together in the garden.

Lizzie was elbow deep in dish washing water when she heard the dining room door close and the sound of footsteps on the tiles in the hallway. Glancing quickly over her shoulder, she saw that Cook and the housekeeper were deep in conversation at the far kitchen table, the remnants of a bottle of wine now poured into two glasses before them.

Silently, doing her utmost not to disturb the two biddies, Lizzie dried her hands on her drying up cloth, and moved towards the kitchen door. Neither woman looked up.

Carefully opening the door, she slipped through into the garden. The night was cold, a bitter wind lifted her hair and ruffled the top of her apron.

"Adam" she whispered.

"I'm here, Lizzie," he said softly.

A tiny red dot glowed in the darkness. She heard him exhale smoke and then draw on his pipe again.

Coming alongside him, she whispered, "I'm pleased to see you. I was worried you may have caught the influenza. it's more than two weeks since you were here."

He gave a chuckle. "I didn't know you were counting, Lizzie."

Lizzie gave him a playful pat. "Don't be bold, Adam." She grinned.

He caught her arm and then frowned. "Lizzie, you are thinner than ever. Do they feed you at all here?"

"Yes, course they do," she lied. Afraid if she complained, she would lose her place in the house and have no roof over her head.

Sounding concerned, he said, "I hope they do. You are a growing girl."

She tried to sound sunny. "I don't think I have much more growing to do. I reckon this is as tall as I will ever be."

In her mind was the disconcerting thought about the changes her body was rapidly going through. There was no one she could confide in and ask advice.

An image of Granny Eliza came into her mind and she sighed inwardly. Granny Eliza would explain everything. If only she could go to her but she couldn't. How could she ever tell Granny Eliza that her own parents had stolen the house the old woman had lived most of her life in.

"Big sigh, Lizzie."

Lizzie was unaware that she had sighed.

Smiling, she said, "More of a shiver than a sigh."

"You go back inside," he said touching her cold hand.

"I'm all right for a moment."

"Sunday," he said. "Do you think you could get the afternoon off and meet me in the park?"

Her eyes glistened in the dark. "I can try."

"I'll wait for you at the old bandstand."

"If I can manage it. I will be there about three o'clock. I'll have to wait until Sunday dinner is over and the dishes are done."

"You work too hard, Lizzie. Perhaps it wasn't the best idea to get you a job with my aunt."

"Don't be silly, Adam. It is fine. I needed a roof over my head. Remember?"

"Yes, I remember, Lizzie. But all the same…"

"Stop worrying, Adam."

She glanced towards the kitchen window, glowing with lamplight. "I must go back in. They'll miss me soon."

He shook spent tobacco from his now cold pipe. "Me too. Uncle will be wondering where I have got to, I am supposed to be making an impression on a potentially important new customer."

Half turning from him, she said, "See you on Sunday, all being well."

"Bye, Lizzie. Take care of yourself."

Opening the back door, she glanced back to where he stood, but the place was empty but for the dark shadows.

"Bye, Adam," she whispered into the blackness.

Slipping into the kitchen, she glanced towards the two women at the table but neither looked up. Relieved, Lizzie stuck her hands into the still warm water and began to scour a roasting pan.

It was late when she eventually got to her small bedchamber in the attic. Taking off her uniform she flung it across the bottom of the bed and climbed in beneath the linen sheets and grey woollen blankets. Her head hardly reached the pillow before she was fast asleep.

Chapter Thirteen

December 1880-December 1881

Christmas arrived with very little fanfare. In her heart of hearts Lizzie was disappointed. She had hoped the big house would be filled with Christmas joy. Perhaps they would decorate, or even have a tree!

She had heard from Bridget, the parlour maid that in some other big houses everybody in the whole house got a gift from the tree. But the grand house was bare of decorations.

Lizzie reflected that she should have been grateful, for if there had been parties and guests then Lizzies work would have been thrice what it was what with the scrubbing and the cleaning and lighting of fires.

Usually there wasn't much of anything delectable left over after Cook and upper staff had eaten.

But the goose was so appetizing Lizzie couldn't take her eyes from it, and Cook took pity on her and told her she would have her share later, and even some of the plum pudding too.

Christmas night, after her work was done, when Lizzie ate her portion, she savoured the rich food, promising herself when she found her sisters, she would cook them the fattest goose that ever was and they would have a tree with decorations, gifts and oranges.

But throughout the days leading to Christmas, Christmas day, and after, it rained and sleeted the entire time and the house felt cold and damp.

Lizzie replenished fires several times a day but it was hard to banish the chill from the bones of the house and the sullenness of the occupants within, who never spared a joy filled minute for the season, but were counting the weeks until the first flower would show it's face through snowdrifts, or through the mire the snow left behind when a thaw set in.

In the months following Christmas, Mrs Lynch did not improve and would declare herself ill, remaining confined to her room for days at a time.

Lizzie had to see to the fire long into the night, running up and down the stairs with chamber pots and buckets of hot water for her to bathe in to restore her equilibrium.

With Mrs Lynch having bouts of illness, invitations to dine or to play cards stalled and no guests appeared to bring a touch of cheerfulness to the sombre atmosphere.

Mr Lynch dined alone in the breakfast room every morning and again in the evening.

Lizzie missed seeing Adam. Often times weeks passed before he came to the house, and when he did come, moods were serious with Adam and his uncle disappearing into the library to discuss business.

On the occasions that he did visit the house and she slipped out to the garden to see him when he smoked, she learned that Adam had been given greater responsibilities.

Now he was the warehouse manager. "It's a good position Lizzie" he had told her, "I am learning a great deal about the business—as I hoped I would—all those years ago when Uncle grudgingly took me on."

Now, Adam knew not only how to organise a warehouse, but where to source the best fabrics, who would pay the best prices, and who might try to undercut him. And he was up on the new trends in textiles, knowing exactly which materials were gaining favour with the wealthy and aristocrats.

Adam's life seemed far more satisfying that her own, and she was happy for him,.

~ ~ ~ ~ ~

As Autumn moved into winter and December arrived, it remained as dull and joyless in the Lynch household, as it had been the previous year with not even a hint of gladness to warm the sullen home.

It was in this solemn state of affairs that Brigid suddenly resigned her position, having been recommended for one closer to her parents, and Lizzies duties were increased.

Although they had not been close, at least Bridget had given Lizzie a friendly smile as they passed in the hallways. But now, it fell to Lizzie to wait upon Mrs Lynch, if Mrs Halbard could not, and since Mrs Lynch had taken to her bed again and Lizzie had to keep the fire going in her room, as well as tend to her, it seemed like there was barely space for Lizzie to even breathe.

How I miss you Granny Eliza, Lizzie breathed into her pillow one cold December night. Although they hadn't had much, Christmas was always something to look forward to with chatter that centred around goose, plum pudding and mince pies.

And each year there would always be an orange from the butcher. Granny Eliza would bring her hoop out for decoration, and Tom would bring holly and red ribbon on Christmas Eve, and they would enjoy fruit cake and sack.

Lying awake, wondering if her life would ever be happy again, she thought of her sisters and swallowed back the lump that formed in her throat.

Imagining them on the streets was too painful to dwell on, and she pushed the thought away. Under the care of their parents, there was little doubt their lives were miserable ones. At least for Lizzie, there would be food tomorrow and a warm dry bed.

God, watch over of my sisters, grant them safety and if it pleases you to do so, please let me find them one day so that we might be together again.

Lizzie didn't pray often, but at Christmas, even in the bleakest of houses, Lizzie thought God seemed a little bit closer. But she knew in her heart of hearts, it would require a miracle for Lizzie to find and rescue her sisters. She turned over and cried. Eventually, somehow, sleep found her.

It was in the fortnight before Christmas when Joshua Lynch returned home unexpectedly. The brass knocker had sounded, and before Jones could fully open the door, Joshua clamped a firm hand on Jones shoulder, flinging the front door wide and standing in the middle of the hall, shouting loudly for his mother to attend the returning hero.

The little brass bell on the board in the kitchen rang frantically.Instantly, Mrs Halbard's and Cook's faces were wreathed in smiles. Lizzie glanced up at it but did not need to be told that Mrs Lynch was demanding attention.

Mrs Halbard ran to attend, but not before stopping in the hallway to welcome Mr Joshua home.

"Where's my mother," he asked cheerfully. "Not like Mama to be absent when I arrive."

"We were not expecting you, Mr Joshua," Mrs Halbard said a little giddily, as Joshua wound her in an embrace.

He laughed. "I have beaten my letter and arrived before it."

"Where is Mama?"

"She has been a little unwell and is in her bedchamber, Mr Joshua. I'm sure your presence in the house will cheer her and she will be her old self in no time."

The bell jangled again and she moved toward the stairs "I must go at once," she said already going up the steps faster than usual.

Picking up the hard packed canvas bag off the floor where he flung it on arriving in the hall, he followed her up.

"I'll put this in my room and then come immediately to see her."

"Oh, Mr Joshua, your room is not ready. I will send Straine to attend to it at once."

"No hurry, Mrs Halbard," he said cheerfully. "I'll see Mama and then enjoy a calming whiskey in the drawing room."

On seeing her son, Mrs Lynch brightened immediately and was well enough to dress and prepare to go downstairs to enjoy a glass of brandy.

Coming downstairs, Joshua went into the withdrawing room and poured a large glass of his father's best whiskey. Sitting beside the blazing fire, he drank slowly, meditating on his journey home and the voyage just completed. His ship was docked in Portsmouth and he wasn't expected to join her until the day after boxing day.

Mrs Halbard came down the stairs somewhat flustered. Rushing into the kitchen she went straight to Lizzie.

"Straine you must prepare Mr Joshua's room. Make up the bed. Light a good fire and polish the furniture. I want a jug of water put on the washstand and a clean towel to hand. Do you understand?"

"Yes, Mrs Halbard."

Ringing her hands, Mrs Halbard paced to the range. "It is such a pity Bridget has left us. She would know exactly how to manage the room..." she turned to Lizzie. "You will just have to do, Straine," she said rudely. "Sows ears never make silk purses, but we must manage with what we have."

Yes, we must, Lizzie thought and restrained the urge to smirk as she allowed her mind to turn Mrs Halbard's face into a grunting, puckered, sow's head.

"Go at once, girl. Light the fire. Air the room. Get fresh linen."

Taking off her clean apron, Lizzie donned the stained one she used for fetching coal, wood, and lighting fires. Leaving the house she went out to the coalhouse and filled a bucket to the brim with coal.

Inside the house once more she struggled up the backstairs of the servants" quarters, and coming to the door that separated the servants from the family, she went through and headed for Mr Joshua's bedchamber.

The chimney was cold and the fire took time to draw properly. When she was satisfied it would catch, she took off her dirty apron, washed her hands in water in her own room and fetched clean linen from the press in the linen cupboard.

She was putting the finishing touches on the room and shining the looking glass, when Mr Joshua opened the door and came in.

His face was slightly pink from the heat of the withdrawing room fire and the two glasses of whiskey he had enjoyed.

Lizzie gave a slight curtsey. "Welcome home, Sir."

"I'm glad to be back." Sighing, he fell onto the bed. "Nothing quite like a proper bed."

He patted the mattress. "Come here girl and give this wandering soul a kiss."

Lizzie felt her cheeks colour and dropped her eyes to the floor.

"That's not the response I usually get. Girls are usually happy to see me."

"I must get back to the kitchen, Sir."

"Come now, Straine. There's nothing that can't wait a few minutes for the sake of welcoming home the young Mister of the house." Standing, he came to her and put his hands on her thin shoulders. "What's your name? I know it isn't just Straine but that is all I get to hear."

Tilting his head slightly to one side, he said, "What is it?"

The blood rushed up Lizzie's neck and burned her cheeks, yet a small smile stole across her lips. Ducking her head to the floor again, she said, "It is Lizzie, Sir."

"Lizzie, Lizzie. Ah yes, I remember it now. A pretty name. It suits you."

"I must be getting back to the kitchen, Sir."

"Off you go, Lizzie."

She turned and was about to open the door when he smacked her bottom.

Lizzie's blush deepened to scarlet.

He laughed out loud. "Lizzie, you redden like a virgin."

Lizzie went through the door quickly and clattered down the back stairs, the bucket rattling in her grip.His behaviour shocked her but in truth, a small part of her was enamoured by the attention. It was such a rarity.

Now Mr Joshua was back, the house had become alive again and Mrs Lynch had ordered the decorations to be unpacked, a tree brought in, and extra candles in the windows.

Mrs Lynch and Halbard discussed the Christmas menu and Lizzie learned that Cook would be roasting something other than goose this year. A turkey had been ordered and it would be served with chestnut stuffing. Lizzie had never in her life known anyone that had even tasted turkey.

As the kitchen hummed and buzzed with excitement, Lizzie began to feel that it really was Christmas again and she felt energised for the first time in an age even though she was working harder than ever.

Over the next day's Mr Joshua's voice could be heard ringing in the hall as he greeted guests.

"Straine," Mrs Halbard called coming into the kitchen where Lizzie was polishing silver. Guests were expected to dinner and she had been informed that she was to wear Bridget's old uniform and bring dishes to the table.

"Straine," Mrs Halbard repeated. "There's to be guests for dinner this evening. I want to show you how and where to lay the dishes when you bring them into the dining room."

Lizzie already knew the next words that would come out of Mrs Halbard's mouth.

"You'll have to do until Mr Lynch replaces Bridget." It was the week before Christmas, and Lizzie doubted that Mr Lynch would be able to hire anyone suitable until after the new year.

Lizzie put aside her polishing rag and followed the housekeeper into the dining room. For the next hour she was drilled into the etiquette expected of a servant. Thoroughly nervous she went to her room in the late afternoon to change into Bridget's uniform. It was too big and it was only with cleverly placed pins that it looked half reasonable.

By five o'clock she was standing in the kitchen for inspection, her fingers trembling slightly and her cheeks flushed with anxiety.

The guests began to arrive and Mrs Halbard showed them into the withdrawing room where Mr Lynch and Joshua awaited. The footman served glasses of champagne for the ladies and whiskey or brandy for the gentlemen.

Coming back into the kitchen, Mrs Halbard ordered Lizzie to go to collect any empty glasses that may be left upon the bookcases or side tables.

Nervous as she had ever been, Lizzie went amongst the guests.

Mr Joshua caught her eye and as she came alongside him to take a glass off the console table, he spoke gently to her. "Don't be afraid, Lizzie. They will not bite you." His voice soothed her and she smiled up into his face.

The dreaded moment when the guests left the withdrawing room and went to the dining room arrived.

Butterflies rose in Lizzie's stomach at the thought that she must carry in the dishes and make no mistakes. Mrs Lynch would dismiss her out of hand should she make an error at the table, or, on entering or leaving the dining room.

The dining room gleamed with candlelight.

Three candelabra blazed with light from four dozen candles on the table set amongst a profusion of holly, mixed with out of season roses and lilies. At the four corners of the room, oil lamps cast a soft glow, the flickering flames breaking the dark shadows.

Carrying a large white soup tureen, Lizzie followed Jones from the kitchen into the dining room and up to the table. Holding firmly to the hot dish, Lizzie watched carefully as Jones served game soup into the soup dishes. Coming to Mr Joshua, Jones spooned a larger portion into his warmed dish. Mr Joshua gave the footman a nod and a smile and then his eyes landed on Lizzie and he smiled anew.

Lizzie purposely looked elsewhere, afraid she may smile.

With the task complete, she was relieved to escape to the safety of the kitchen. Cook was waiting at the cooking range for a report of how the guests had received her game soup.

Whilst vegetables were spooned into warmed tureens, and a large rib of beef was placed on a meat platter, Lizzie went back into the dining room to collect the empty soup dishes.

She felt Mr Joshua's eyes on her and was afraid to look his way, but at the very last second, before she walked away from the table, their eyes met and he smiled warmly.

Lizzie retreated into the kitchen feeling a little confused and wondering why he was being so kind to her. Of course she was flattered, Mr Joshua was always the centre of attention. Everyone wished to be close to him, to feel the spark of his energy and enthusiasm.

Lizzie carried in the vegetable tureens and Mrs Halbard brought in the platter of beef. Joshua rose and going to the sideboard he began to carve the ribs. Lizzie carried around the plates and placed them carefully before each guest.

Two or three hours slipped by, and when the dessert was served, a concoction of aromatic dried fruits from the mystical countries of Joshua's travels—the guests were begging him to bring more back from his next voyage.

Eventually the guests slipped away, melding into the spring night in carriages.

Lizzie, exhausted, slipped off her boots and began to wash the pile of dishes and pots stacked on every available surface in the kitchen.

Cook pleading tiredness was first to leave the kitchen, hastily followed by Mrs Halbard who said her feet were in such a poor state she could no longer bear to stand another moment.

Lizzie plodded on, making room for breakfast to be cooked in the morning.

Lizzie put another kettle of cold water to the flames of the fire to heat.

The door opened and Mr Joshua came in. He was a little drunk, swaggering slightly but his usual smile and good humour was intact.

"Lizzie," he said. "You did a marvellous job tonight."

He grabbed a dishcloth from a pile on the kitchen table. "I'm here to help."

"Oh no, Mr Joshua, you can't possibly do that."

"Yes, I can," he said lifting a plate from the stack near the sink.

He began to wipe it furiously and Lizzie feared for the plate.

"I thought you had come into the kitchen for a cake or a biscuit," she said looking up into his face.

He gave the plate another wipe with the cloth. "I couldn't eat another thing. Dinner was delicious but there was a lot of it."

She glanced at him and then put her hands back into the washing up water.

Putting the plate aside, he came up behind her and kissed the back of her neck.

It tickled and Lizzie flinched. "You mustn't do that, Mr Joshua."

"Why not?"

"Because it isn't right."

"What do you mean, it is not right? It is what men and women do. You have been leading me on for the past days and yet you refuse me."

A sense of panic swept over Lizzie. "No. I have not led you on at all. You've been kind to me. That is all. And if I gave you any wrong ideas—"

"Well I will darn well have my due. I have held back but now I will wait no longer."

An image of Adam's kind face leapt into Lizzie mind. She pushed Joshua Lynch back.

Grabbing her skirt, tearing the waistband, he yanked it up.

As he suspected, Lizzie wore no drawers, maids rarely did. Holding her firmly against the sink, he unbuttoned his breeches and entered her roughly and brutishly.

Lizzie cried out in pain. Too shocked to fight back, she cried out but there was no one awake to hear her pitiful calls.

He was gone in a moment, slamming the kitchen door behind him. Slipping to the floor, Lizzie cried bitter tears.

An hour went by before she rose. Holding the tatters of her borrowed uniform, she climbed the servants" quarters to her solitary bed.

Without a doubt Mrs Halbard would want the uniformed returned tomorrow. By the light of a single candle, Lizzie repaired the damage to the skirt. Her tears like rain on a windowpane blinding her to the task.

Two hours later, Lizzie rose from her bed, she had not slept at all, and went down the stairs to rake out the fire and light the ones needed, afresh.

The next day Mr Joshua was aloof and did not attempt any kindness with Lizzie. Burning with shame, she attempted to stay away from any areas of the house where she might encounter him. Meal times were agonising as she had no choice but to pass by him as she cleared dishes from the table.

On Christmas day, Lizzie woke especially early and went downstairs to begin her duties without a modicum of joy for the day. Uncharacteristically Cook was already in the kitchen, and barked orders at Lizzie the moment she laid eyes on her. "Get a move on Straine—I'll need you back in here right quick, to help with the vegetables."

Lizzie raked and cleaned and lit the fireplaces, scrubbed and polished and then returned to the kitchen to help with the festive foods. Even when she had been a small child with her parents, she had never hated Christmas. She had wished for things, but never hated the day.

By seven o'clock guests were arriving and Lizzie heard the sound of the sharp brass knocker and Adam and his mother were announced.

As she waited the dinner table with Jones that night, Adam tried to catch her eye, but she could not look at him. Mr Joshua was the perfect gentlemen all evening, charming, and entertaining and though Lizzie did not desire kind and friendly gestures it seemed Lizzie may have been invisible to him, and of no consequence whatsoever. She burned with shame and fury.

By days end, when the last dishes had been done, Lizzie retrieved her Christmas dinner plate and ate it mindlessly, unable to notice the sumptuous flavours.

Earlier, when Adam had gone into the garden to smoke, she had not been able to bring herself to join him, so he had visited the kitchen briefly, and delivered a package of Bon-Bons to the staff, looking directly to Lizzie. It might well have been intended for her alone, but now Cook had appropriated the package.

A few days after Christmas, and before the new year. The house was deathly quiet. Mr Joshua had left the house for his ship, slipping away in the darkness and headed for Portsmouth. Distance and his ship would hide his crime against an innocent girl.

Chapter Fourteen

February 1882

Weeks went by and the sense of shame stalked Lizzie every hour of the day, the nightmare only loosening its grip when she fell into an exhausted sleep in her solitary bed at night.

Mr and Mrs Lynch, seemed exhausted by their son's visit and shunned invitations to dine out and received not a single visitor in their home for several weeks.

It was with mixed feeling that she learned from Mrs Halbard that Adam was to dine at his uncle's house on the following evening.

Lizzie was in turmoil. Should she seek Adam out when she had the chance? If she told him what had happened, he might blame her, for he seemed firm friends with Mr Joshua. And Joshua Lynch was his cousin after all. Lizzie would lose her position immediately and she would lose Adam's friendship.

Lizzie agonized over the shame of what Mr Joshua had done. Had she been guilty of what Mr Joshua had said? Had she led Mr Joshua to believe she was willing? How could she face Adam in any manner? What would Adam think of her now? Would he look at her with kindness in his eyes, ever again.

No, the more likely scenario was that Lizzie would be seen as responsible for what had occurred, and sullied goods.

What was she to do? She would shun Adam, yes, that seemed the best option. She would not seek him out in the garden as she usually did, as she had always done. It was, she decided, the only course of action open to her.

At six o'clock on the dot, Adam arrived and was ushered into the withdrawing room by Jones. From her place in the kitchen, standing at the sink washing pots, Lizzie heard his voice as he entered the foyer and a burst of his laughter before the withdrawing room door closed.

A wave of loneliness swept through her and she choked her tears back. How she longed to confide in him. To hear him insist that the awful thing that had happened to her was not her fault.

Later, when she saw the glow of his pipe in the garden, when she did not slip away to meet him, but remained in the kitchen, away from the windows, the sorrow and shame sent waves of nausea through her, and she swallowed the bile that rose from her belly.

He had always shown her kindness and friendship and now she was repaying him with cruel indifference. But that was better than if he knew her shame.

Eventually Adam's footfalls sounded on the tiled floor in the hall. The front door opened and closed and then there was silence. She had made her choice. She could not confide in Adam and she could not face Adam. She would not seek him out again. When the time came that she would be required to wait on him in the dining room, she would remain aloof. From now on, he would never be part of her life again.

Though there had been periods in her life of great sadness, she felt that losing Adam's friendship was the worst she had suffered thus far.

Crying herself to sleep in her chill bed, she awoke in the early hours, her pillow still damp with her tears. At five o'clock she rose and dressed quickly. There were fires to rake out and lay afresh, chamber pots to empty and rinse, pots and pans to scrub and all the endless tasks that would fill her day until she retired at nine o'clock that night.

Bone tired, she opened the door of her tiny bedchamber and went down the servants stairs to begin her day.

A few hours later, she carried a serving dish of mutton chops and devilled kidneys into the breakfast room.

As she came into the room, she saw Mr and Mrs Lynch sitting at the table. Mrs Lynch was opening a letter with a silver letter opener. Ignoring the servant's necessary intrusion, Mrs Lynch pulled a sheet of paper out of the envelope.

A smile brightening her face, as she said, "Darling Joshua is in Spain. Isn't that marvellous. He is enjoying wonderful weather and wine." She chortled. "It seems there is a very charming senorita to keep him company. Joshua, Joshua, what a boy you are." She tittered.

Lizzie felt vaguely nauseous at the mention of Mr Joshua's name.

Putting the dish down with a clatter, she hurried out of the room and ran to the kitchen and dashed to the back door.

The cold breeze caught her breath. Bile rose in her throat and before she had got beyond the terrace, she was overcome with nausea and although she had eaten nothing, she was violently sick.

It took several moments to recover but once she felt a little better she headed back to the kitchen. Coming into the warm and steamy atmosphere, she immediately felt ill again. Cook tossed a fish in the skillet and the aroma of fish frying sent her outdoors again.

As the door slammed behind her, Mrs Halbard looked to cook. "What is that all about?"

"I don't know but it isn't the first time this week that Straine has made a dash to be outdoors.

Mrs Halbard frowned.

The two women were waiting for her to come indoors.

Lizzie already suspected that she may be pregnant. Missing her monthly curse and feeling nauseous every day was exactly how her mother suffered when she had been expecting.

The idea of pregnancy and a baby terrified her. She was certain to lose her place with the Lynch family and be made homeless with no one to turn to for help. Her parents, even if she could find them, would offer nothing but advice of how she could make a living on the streets as a prostitute.

Adam was lost to her forever. She would never forgive herself for that.

Mrs Lynch was unlikely to welcome her grandchild into a happy home. Joshua would deny all knowledge. No one would believe her.

Mrs Halbard was the first to speak. Harshly, she shouted, "Straine, what do you have to say for yourself?"

Lizzie looked to the toecaps of her boots showing beneath the hem of her uniform skirt.

"Look at me you hussy," Mrs Halbard shrieked.

Tears filled Lizzie eyes.

Cook sighed. She was not a soft and kindly woman, having many times given Lizzie the harsh edge of her tongue. But she was in some small ways, a fair woman, making sure there was at least some food left over for Lizzie at night. Now, an uncharacteristic sadness deepened the lines over Cook's face.

Mrs Halbard frowned deeply. "Go upstairs. Take off your uniform and put on the garments you arrived in, when you came to this respectable house looking for work, which Mr Lynch so generously provided you, when you had not even a letter to recommend you. Be gone immediately. I'll have no truck with the likes of you bringing shame to a good Christian family."

The tears overflowed and Lizzie's cheeks were wet.

"Go. What are you standing there for?"

Wiping her face with the back of her hands, Lizzie walked to the door and passed through, clattering up the back stairs to her small attic bedchamber.

"Who do you think could have got her in this way?" Cook said putting the kettle to the back of the range. "She never goes out."

Mrs Halbard harrumphed. She had an idea who the culprit was but if it was true, Lizzie Straine must have led him on. She'd hear no bad things said about Mr Joshua Lynch. He was a good man. Though he was a man and men were sometimes overcome with undesirable and primeval needs.

Taking off the uniform dress, Lizzie flung it onto the floor in rage. Her old dress was too short and showed the tops of her boots. It was also too big in the bodice and gaped at the neck and beneath the arms.

Flustered, face still wet with tears, she wrapped the green shawl Granny Eliza had knitted for her and tied it tightly. Her coat was in the wooden coffer, the only piece of furniture in the room, beside the bed. Taking out her old coat she put it on. There was a sinking feeling in her stomach.

Where was she to go? There would be no Granny Eliza to rescue her this time. Going to the door, she glanced back into the room, and then walked down the stairs.

There was no avoiding Mrs Halbard, she was waiting at the foot of the stairwell. Her face red with anger.

"I want you gone as far away from this house as possible. I will not have the good name of Mr and Mrs Lynch sullied by the likes of you."

Her anger bubbled over and she struck Lizzie's cheek viciously, leaving a red imprint of her palm.

Lizzie shrieked in pain and surprise.

Mrs Halbard grabbed her coat collar, catching up tresses of Lizzie's hair and dragged her into the kitchen. The outside door was already open and thrusting Lizzie towards it, she threw her out. Lizzie landed heavily on the paving stones.

"Good riddance," Mrs Halbard shouted as she slammed the door closed.

Picking herself up, Lizzie shook debris off the skirt of her coat. Her face stung unmercifully but she wouldn't put her hand to it, she had too much pride for that, especially as Mrs Halbard was watching her through the window, with a satisfied smirk on her face.

Lizzie couldn't wait to put distance between her and the Lynch household. Walking quickly, she went in the opposite direction to Adam's place of work and kept walking until her legs ached with the effort.

Reaching a park, she went through the gates and walked slowly along a narrow pathway until she came to a wooden bench. Sitting, she sighed with relief and tiredness.

What was she to do? Prostitution? The workhouse? Become a thief, grabbing what she could of market stalls to survive— risking prison every day?

It didn't bear thinking about. There was no point looking for another place to work as a scullery or kitchen maid, she had no reference. Nobody would employ her without one. She glanced down at her belly.

It wouldn't be too long before everyone would learn of her shame. No prospect of a job with a baby on the way. Hungry and thirsty she got up off the bench and went out of the park. She had noticed a workman's café. She would get a cup of tea and then decide what she was to do.

The atmosphere in the café was steamy and the place smelled of fried meat. Lizzie felt her stomach roil and swallowed several times to bury the nausea.

Getting a mug of hot tea at the counter, she took it to a corner table to drink it.

The place was full of workmen, in their dirty work clothes. Most were uncouth, spitting in spittoons and wiping their noses on the cuffs of their coats.

Lizzie tried to look away, but her eyes kept coming back to them. If she took up prostitution these were the type of men that would pay pennies to use her body. Parting her legs with their dirty hands, and worse. The thought was revolting.

An image of Joshua Lynch came into her mind, his clean hands lifting her skirt and she shuddered at the dreadful memory.

No! Prostitution was not an easy way out. Harder probably than the workhouse. Though she felt faint at the thought of going to the dreaded place, there was a workhouse on Cleveland Street—the Strand Union Workhouse. P

erhaps they would take her in as she had lived in the parish. It was a long walk, nearer to the old place she had shared with Granny Eliza than the Lynch house she had just left.

~ ~ ~ ~ ~

The Strand looked as fearsome as she imagined it to be. The austere building was shadowed by warehouses and tenements. Lizzie remembered shivering with dread as Granny Eliza had spoken of it. Now she was here herself, looking for shelter. How far she had slipped since the night Joshua Lynch had come into the kitchen and lifted her skirt.

Lizzie shuddered remembering some of the tales Granny Eliza and even her own mother had told of the place. She could only hope things had changed since Granny Eliza had a brush with the workhouse, her sister being an occupant there for a while. At that time five-hundred people were housed within.

Looking at the place now, Lizzie wondered how they managed to cram in so many. Here was where they hid away the elderly, the sick, the broken and the poor women who had the misfortune to be pregnant and unmarried.

Amidst all the suffering were the lunatics, chained to their beds. Granny Eliza swore her sister was put on a starvation diet for being unmarried after she gave birth, here in this dreadful place.

Lizzie sighed for the inmates of the past, glad they at least had the good Doctor Rogers to make some improvements. The chains were replaced with leather bonds and the new mothers were at least given food. The doctor had gone over the heads of the workhouse master and his wife. Granny Eliza said it must have taken bravery to do that.

Gathering her courage she went to the closed door and rattled the brass knocker.

The door opened and a hag of a woman stood on the threshold. Lizzie was tempted to run but the thought of being outdoors throughout the night kept her rooted to the ground.

"Yes," the grey haired elderly woman said sharply.

Lizzie had no idea what to answer and spoke the first words that came into her head. "I'm looking for shelter. I am of the parish."

The woman glanced at Lizzie's worn clothes and Lizzie guessed she was assessing her ability to work.

The door opened enough to allow Lizzie to pass through. There was no lamp light nor firelight to give the large hall a glimmer of warmth. The windows were shadowed by tall building that stole the light. It was as cold indoors as it was out.

She was aware there was a hum of noise coming from within the house and every few moments it was punctuated by a loud shriek and a sound like someone banging a tin cup.

Lizzie shivered. Were the lunatics still kept here? It was a question she was afraid to ask the disgruntled woman standing beside her.

"I'll get someone to show you to the female dormitory. You have missed the evening meal. You will have to go hungry until tomorrow evening. If you are lucky you may get a bit of bread in the morning. Depends if there is enough to go around."

A woman came through a large door at the far end of the hallway and approached fearfully.

"Miss Harper," she said in a plaintive voice.

"What is it, Maddock?"

"I need a little gruel for my son but no one in the kitchen will give me some."

"Then he will have to go without."

"But Miss Harper, he is very hungry."

The elderly woman's hand snaked out and she clouted the woman on the side of the face.

Lizzie jumped back in surprise.

"Now, go, Maddock. Don't let me see you in the hallway again. Do you understand?"

Clutching her face, her lip split, the woman darted back beyond the door that was still ajar.

Lizzie felt as though she had entered a nightmare.

The Strand Union Workhouse was everything that Lizzie had feared it would be. The days began at four-thirty in the morning and finished in the evening with a watery dish of gruel.

Miss Harper had put Lizzie to work with the poor people who had lost their minds and those so old they were no longer continent. Though she did her best it was impossible not to be sickened by the work she endured.

Chapter Fifteen

Tired to the bones of her body, Lizzie rose out of her bed just before four-thirty. The room was cold and the icy draught from beneath the door chilled her bare feet. Shivering she reached for her green shawl and flung it over her shoulder.

The water in the jug on the dresser was freezing cold, pouring a little into the chipped and crazed basin, she doused her hands and face and then dried them on a threadbare towel.

Dressing quickly and donning her old boots, she was ready to go downstairs. There was always a chance she would get a mug of lukewarm tea and a slice of bread in the communal dining room. She joined the queue, guessing there were probably a hundred people in front of her.

More inmates joined the line and the low hum of their voices sounded like bees around a honey pot.

That so many people, made so little noise, wasn't surprising. There was little to talk about beside the day ahead or the one just gone.

The snaking line moved slowly and Lizzie, depressed and unhappy, felt the apathy and misery leaching from everybody around her.

Eventually her turn came and she collected a mug with a little tea from the dirty hand of a fellow inmate. The bread had run out, there was no point complaining so she moved forward and sat on the end of a wooden bench, her hands around the tepid mug. Swallowing the watery tea, she thought of her day ahead and tears filmed her eyes. Yet the thought of her early morning chores — to change the beds soiled overnight by the bedridden and senile occupants— made her queasy stomach, turn over again.

An image of Adam came to her and she imagined walking with him through the park on a winter's afternoon. It was hard to accept she would never see him again.

A harsh voice broke into her reverie, "Straine. Get a move on."

Lizzie rose like an old woman and went towards the door, resigned to the dreadful chores ahead of her.

The stink in the men's dormitory was overpowering and as she entered, Lizzie gagged. Turning quickly, she vomited into a basin of water.

"Hope you are not in the family way," a female inmate said.

"No." Lizzie lied.

"Good. For sure as hell they'll snatch your new baby and sell it to the first person that wants it."

It was impossible not to touch her still flat stomach and think of the life already growing there.

Several beds were changed, and the occupants cleaned, by Lizzie and another young girl. The girl was pregnant and the birth of her baby was clearly imminent. Feeling sorry for her, Lizzie offered to take the soiled sheets down to the old barn, where cauldrons simmered over open fires.

The place stank of excrement. Dropping the load of filthy linen beside a steaming metal tub, Lizzie made a quick retreat. Only stopping for a moment by a basin of cold water to clean her hands.

Her stomach roiled, still nauseas from the stench of the bedding. If she could just get a cup of tea, weak as it would be, it would help. Maybe one of the girls would take pity on her. Lizzie went through the back door of the workhouse and towards the vast kitchen. The thought of the tea encouraged her, but there would be consequences if she was caught out of her area.

As she passed by the door leading to the entrance hall, she heard raised voices, a female and a male. She was just about to make a dash for the kitchen door, when she distinctly heard Adam's voice

"I want to see her now," his voice was raised and worried. "I need to know she is safe."

Lizzie heard the voice of the workhouse principle's wife. It was clipped, with an unkind, dangerous, edge of command. Although Lizzie could leave anytime, so she had been led to believe, the workhouse sold the labour of the many poor souls that had no other option for survival, and much of the money never reached the official coffers of the workhouse.

"The inmates are not allowed to have visitors. So please leave immediately."

"Lizzie Straine," Adam was shouting, "will not be an inmate in this hell hole for a moment longer. Now tell me where to find her."

Opening the door, Lizzie entered the hallway.

Adam's face lit on seeing her. "Lizzie," he shouted.

"Oh, Adam," she cried.

"Straine, get back to work immediately," Mistress Harper shrieked. "I will not tolerate such insubordination. Do you hear me?"

Lizzie was torn between staying with Adam and obeying the woman, but she moved towards the open door to obey Mistress Harper. Adam covered the distance in a flash.

Catching her arm, he said, "Lizzie you do not have to go back in there."

"I have nothing, Adam. Nowhere to stay. No work. Nothing."

"I will take care of everything, Lizzie. There is nothing to fear."

"I will not tell you again, Straine. Get back to work."

Lizzie glanced into Adam's eyes."

"Lizzie," he said softly. "Come with me. Everything will be sorted out. I promise you."

"Lizzie, I will take you away from here and take care of you. You don't need to stay here."

A smile flitted across her lips and then her chin began to tremble.

"Do you have things you want to bring with you?"

"Just my coat, shawl and old dress."

Releasing her arm, he said, "Good, go now and get them."

He caught her hand and held it firmly. "On second thoughts. Do not go alone. I will come with you. I do not trust the people here."

Mrs Harper shouted, "That's preposterous. A man cannot go to the female dormitory."

Ignoring her, Adam opened the door and followed Lizzie through it.

Dashing to it, Mrs Harper shouted at the retreating figures, "There will be compensation to pay."

Lizzie flinched and she stopped in her tracks.

Turning, Adam said, "I do not doubt it, madam. How much is it?"

"A guinea," Mrs Harper shouted. "A guinea."

"Money very well spent, Mrs Harper."

In an instant, Adam placed a guinea in her outstretched palm.

Without a word passing between them, Adam followed Lizzie as she went to the female dorm, gathered her old coat and her green shawl. Together they walked out of the dormitory, out through the entrance, and through the gates.

As she stood on the outside of the gates, Lizzie breathed in the foetid London air and felt more free than she had ever felt. She did not notice the putrid odours. To Lizzie, the air could not have been fresher.

"When did you last eat, Lizzie?"

"Yesterday," she said matter-of-factly as though not eating was just a minor inconvenience.

"There's a café nearby. We will go there and you can eat and relax."

He gave her a worried sidelong glance. "Lizzie you look all in."

"I am tired," she said softly.

The delicious aroma of mutton and ham being fried, and the sound of eggs splattering in a pan, was for a moment overwhelming for Lizzie when she and Adam entered the café. Lizzie realised she hadn't had a meal that didn't consist of watery gruel and dried bread in her entire time at the workhouse. She felt famished and empty and longed for a proper cup of tea.

Adam led her to a table in the corner of the room and Lizzie sank gratefully onto a wooden seat there.

"I will order some food. Would you like tea to start off with?"

"Yes, please Adam." How nice it was to have someone take charge and take care of her.

While he was at the counter ordering food, Lizzie began to worry about her immediate future. Where was she to stay? She had little money and no prospect of a job.

He came back carrying two full mugs of hot tea and put them down. Lizzie took hers up immediately.

When the plates of food arrived, Lizzie was amazed at the size of the meal, never before had she seen so much on her plate. The cost of it worried her.

Guessing what was in her mind, Adam said, "Just eat, Lizzie. If you don't you will fall between the cracks in the pavement and disappear altogether."

Picking up her fork, she laughed. The sound was almost new to her, it had been a while since she had laughed. Not since the dreadful night Joshua Lynch had lifted her skirt. How was she to explain to Adam that she was expecting a baby? He would surely abandon her entirely and she would be on the streets and alone.

"I can see by the frown on your face that you are concerned and worrying about something, Lizzie. Will you just eat? Everything can be sorted. Rarely are things as bad as they seem. Trust me, Lizzie. Please trust me."

Hiding tears, Lizzie cut into the hot egg, watching the perfect yellow yolk flow onto a slice of crisped ham.

When the meal was over, he led her to a boarding house and booked a room for her. Going into it for the first time, Lizzie was amazed at the pleasant space and modern furniture.

"Adam this is too much. I cannot pay you back."

He took both her hands in his. "Lizzie, stop worrying."

"But I have to worry," she said plaintively.

"No you do not. We can find another position for you. A better one."

"I don't have a testimonial, Adam." Tears flooded her eyes. "No one will take me on without a testimonial from my previous place of work. Oh Adam, I'm lost."

Her tears touched him. Moved, he put his arm around her shoulder and drew her close. "All will be well, Lizzie."

The warmth of his body comforted her and she was tempted to lay her head on his shoulder and let the rare feeling of safety envelop her. Instead she sniffed back the tears and stood straight.

"Lizzie I want you to catch up on your sleep. I will come tomorrow evening to see you. Until then please do not agonise over your future. We will find a solution."

Reaching out to her, he lifted her small chin with the tip of his finger. "Promise me you will try to rest. I will be back before dark tomorrow and we can talk again."

She gave a weak smile. "I will do as you say, Adam."

He pressed some coins to her hand and then closed the door behind him. She listened to his footfall on the wooden stairs, and then the front door opened and closed and he was gone.

Suddenly Lizzie felt alone. Looking through the window she saw him hurrying up the road and then he was lost to her as a horse drawn vehicle came to a standstill at the curb side. When the vehicle moved on, there was no sight of him. Lizzie sighed.

She meant to sit on the bed for just a few moments but several hours went by before the sound of knocking on the door awakened her. Disorientated she looked to the window and saw the evening sky was darkening. Rising quickly, expecting to see Adam on the threshold, she opened the door.

The lady of the house beamed a smile at her. Lizzie caught the aroma of beef and realised she was hungry. "Your companion asked me to deliver supper to you at six o'clock." The woman held out a laden tray for Lizzie to take.

Still half asleep, Lizzie took it. "That is very kind of you."

The woman straightened her mop cap. "Eat it while it is hot. Humming a little tune, the landlady started down the stairs, her boots drumming on the wooden treads.

Closing the door with a nudge of her hip, Lizzie put the tray down on the bed. Uncovering a basin she saw a delicious meal of beef broth and suet dumplings. Taking up the spoon beside it, she began eating hungrily.

When she had finished, she carried the tray down stairs and knocked on the landlady's door. As she climbed the stairs again, exhaustion hit her anew.

Undressing, she climbed between the sheets, yet worn and weary as she was, she lay worrying about her future and that of her unborn child. Somewhere in the night sleep found her, and Lizzie woke to the sound of the pigeons perched on the windowsill, cooing at sunrise.

At ten o'clock she came out of her room and headed for the street.

Deprived of fresh air and open spaces for so long she wanted to make the most of a day of freedom, putting her problems to the back of her mind for a little while.

Though the local park was small, she wandered there for a while, taking in the scent of the bushes and shrubs, only leaving it for a cup of tea in a small café in the early afternoon.

As good as his word, Adam arrived at the boarding house before dark. Flying up the stairs two at a time, he knocked on her bedchamber door.

"Lizzie," he said as she opened the door. "You look so much better already."

"I had a very long sleep and spent the day outdoors, so I feel so much better. I have been tired for so long, I had forgotten what it is like not to be." She smiled and her face lit.

"I hope you are hungry," he said returning the smile.

"A little," she didn't admit she had not eaten all day, afraid to spend any more of the pennies in her pocket.

"Good. There's a chop-house nearby. They do good food, and there will be plenty."

~ ~ ~ ~ ~

Opening the glass panelled door to the chop house, Adam stood aside for Lizzie to enter. The air was heavy with the smell of frying sausages. Lizzie caught sight of a piece of belly pork coming out of the oven, sizzling hot, on a metal pan.

Adam ordered two portions of the pork. When the plates came to the table, there was a mound of white beans and boiled potatoes to go with the meat.

When the empty plates were removed, Adam said, "Let's go for a walk Lizzie, there are some things I would like to talk about."

Out on the street, they walked slowly, despite the cold, ice covered streets. "I had a little good luck today Lizzie. More than a little in truth, and I have also got you what is rightfully yours.

"What do you mean?"

When I found you had been let go, and where you were. My uncle and I had words, and I told him that it was grossly unfair to let you go without a testimonial.

Lizzie's mouth dropped open. "What did he say?"

Adam grinned. "He muttered a lot and then he went into his office and stayed there for a while."

Putting his hand in his pocket, Adam drew out an envelope. "Eventually he came out with this."

"What is it?"

"Your testimonial, Lizzie."And a thousand pounds.

"A thousand pounds?"

Lizzie started to shake. Why would Mr Lynch provide her such a sum, not unless he was afraid of something, not unless he was forced.

He grinned again. "Yes! I reminded him that you had worked your fingers to the bone for the family with little reward."

Lizzie was barely listening. Her mind was racing and she was in a state of panic. *Does Adam know Joshua Lynch has me pregnant?* Finally not daring to ask, she stammered out, "I hope you didn't risk your position for my benefit."

"No, no.. nothing like that happened. As a matter of fact, Uncle has made me a partner in the business.. He wasn't happy, but he saw the good sense of it in the end, especially since his son doesn't know the slightest thing about business."

Lizzie looked at him, wide eyed. *What could he mean? Why is he talking about Joshua Lynch?*

"If I chose, I could take Uncle's customers — it wouldn't be so difficult for me to find an investor should I decide to become his business rival, so he wisely, chose to accept my words."

What words?

"The words that my cousin wronged you Lizzie. And that all that you have endured since you were thrown out of the house is on the head of their son. And that I would make certain it was known, and force a marriage."

"Marriage?"

"Oh don't look so bleak Lizzie, I never would have seen you married to that scoundrel. But if you will have me, I would be a very happy man to be your husband. I've always loved you Lizzie Strain, and when I lost you, I knew there was nothing I would not do to find you again. I just hope you feel the same way as I do." He gave a short nervous cough and then faced her. Taking both her hands in his, he asked her gently, "Lizzie will you be my wife?"

Lifting her face to his, he saw the tears lying on her lashes. He pulled her close to him and hugged her tightly.

"Lizzie, you haven't answered me. I do not blame you at all. I want to marry you and take care of you and the baby."

She held onto his coat, searching his eyes. "Oh, Adam."

"Now shush. You still haven't answered my question. Will you marry me, Lizzie Straine?"

Tears of joy filmed her eyes.

"Yes, my darling Adam. I will marry you."

He held her close. "Good. Now we can start to make plans. We can be married in St. Cuthbert's as soon as I can arrange it. You will need a new coat and dress. Granny Eliza will be happy to help you shop, I'm sure."

"Adam—are you certain, I—"

"Lizzie, hush. I am more than certain I want to spend my life with you by my side, and only glad you will have me."

"Oh Adam, I've been so afraid, and so terribly sad. I thought if you knew what had happened you would never ever look at me again. In a way, I was glad to leave, so I wouldn't have to face you."

Adam held her tight and stroked her hair. "I know you Lizzie. I know you would not have been so imprudent as to take Joshua to your bed. And I would not be speaking the truth, if I did not say, that I know Joshua too."

Finding themselves at the park now, he sat her down on the bench and took her hands.

"I feared something was wrong, when you didn't meet me in the garden, as you usually would.

And so, I resolved to find you the next time I had opportunity. When I found there was a new young maid. I tried to question my aunt but she wouldn't be drawn. After dinner, I approached my uncle in the withdrawing room, he said that you had left to go to another workplace."

Dark anger passed briefly over Adam's face. "As I knew you were settled with my aunt and uncle, my suspicions became really aroused. Going into the kitchen, I spoke to the housekeeper and she confirmed you had gone elsewhere. When she went out of the room, I questioned Cook and she told me the truth. I was livid when she told me what she had seen."

Lizzie's hand flew to her mouth. "Cook knew, really *knew* what happened?"

Adam rubbed her hands between his own. "She was afraid for her job, and she has known Joshua since he was a baby. But once I confronted her the guilt was too much. She had come back to the kitchen for a cup of tea, and when she saw what was happening and how you were crying – she fled."

Lizzie's face grew red with rage and hot tears fell. "The lies and the things she said about me—when all the time.."

Adam shook his head in sorrow and sighed. "Sometimes there's no justice in the world. But not this time Lizzie, this time, you win."

"Yes, I have rather, haven't I," Lizzie beamed through watery eyes. "But how did you find me?"

"And so," Adam continued, "after that, straight away I went to see Tom and Granny Eliza but they knew nothing. Granny Eliza gave me the addresses of laundresses in the district that you may have gone to. I searched but no one knew where you were. As a last resort I went to the Strand Workhouse, and although I hoped not to find you there, I also hoped that I would, so my search would be over. Before I saw the harridan, Mrs Harper, I spoke to the manager, he was unhelpful but when he saw my money he became obliging. And the rest is history, Lizzie."

He put his arm around her shoulder and pulled her a little closer. "Thank goodness I found you. I may have been searching for evermore."

He stood and pulled her up. "We have work to do. We need to visit the vicar at St Cuthberts. We must get a wedding ring. I would like to have a small gathering and a wedding breakfast so we must organise that, if you agree."

"I'm in a whirl, Adam. At this moment I may very well agree to anything."

"Good," he said. "Then we will visit Granny Eliza and Tom and tell them our very good news."

But Lizzie's mood had faltered. Granny Eliza would want an explanation, about everything.

~ ~ ~ ~ ~

Granny Eliza gave a small yelp, when she opened the door to see Lizzie and Adam.

"Oh my girl! Oh my girl! I thought I might have lost you forever. I scanned every corner of my mind thinking where you might go. Come in, come in," she said ushering them through the doorway of Tom's house.

"Granny Eliza" Lizzie sobbed. "I'm so sorry. I had to leave your house. You don't know what I did."

Granny Eliza held Lizzie at arm's length and beamed at her. "You are skin and bone girl, but We'll soon fix that up. Tom get the cake from the tin and put the kettle on, there's a love."

Old Tom rose from his seat and gave Granny Eliza a soft look as she ran her hands over Lizzies bony frame."

"You mean that your no good parents are living there, drinking and fighting. I saw it for myself child. Your pa let me have a good piece of his mind too when I asked about your whereabouts. I can see they ran you off."

"Oh Granny Eliza, I thought you would be so ashamed of me, after all that you did for me. But it was my sisters. I just wanted to help them. Mam and Pa took all that I had and then the house. There was nothing I could do. I couldn't stand up to them."

"There, there child." Granny Eliza guided her to the small table where Tom had placed bread and cheese, and cake. The kettle steamed as he filled the old tea pot. "It's your poor sisters I'm worried about. I'd have taken "em in if I could have."

"You've seen them? Are they well?"

"Now Lizzie, you can guess what they're doing can't you?

Lizzie burst into tears anew, she didn't really need Granny Eliza to fill the details of what she instinctively knew. "The youngest one is out begging but your other sister, she's a working girl now."

~ ~ ~ ~ ~

"I can't bear it Adam. I can't bear to think of Martha walking the streets this way. And it will be only a short time before Annie joins her. Lizzie was wringing her hands and pacing.

I have an idea, Adam said. Let me go to your father. I know you don't want to see them, but I don't mind." A steely glint flashed in his eyes.

Lizzie looked at Adam. The years spent unloading and hauling bales of fabrics had given him broad shoulders and a strong back.

"What will you do?"

"Never you be minding what I'll do, but I dare say, they will let your sisters go. Now that you have secured a home, they will be safe."

Lizzie smiled. The money that Mr Lynch had given to Lizzie had been enough to buy a comfortable house and with Adam's help, Lizzie would open her own dressmaking business.

Adam had even secured an agreement with his Uncle, that to help Lizzie become established, he would recommend her as a reputable and clever seamstress, and in return Lizzie would sell her clients on his most costly fabrics.

Adam and Mr Lynch agreed together, that Joshua would never be named under any circumstance.

~ ~ ~ ~ ~

It was two nights later that Adam returned with Martha.

Lizzie's heart soared as Martha ran to her arms. Adam stood off to the side watching.

"Oh Lizzie, I thought I'd never see you again."

Scraping her sister's hair back from her wet, dirty face Lizzie kissed it. "I never gave up trying to find you Martha, you and Annie, I just didn't know how I could save you from him. But it's over now. You're safe and you will live here with me and Adam."

"But what about Pa, he'll look for us for certain."

"Just trust us Martha, Pa won't come looking for you. Adam will make sure. And by the end of the week, we will all be together again."

True to his word, within the week, Adam delivered Annie to Lizzie's new home. A bruise was forming over his cheek and his knuckles were scraped.

When Lizzie asked him about her parents, he merely said "Let sleeping dogs lie Lizzie. But don't you worry they know what will happen if they show up here for any reason." Lizzie nodded.

A part of her wanted to weep for them, but the joy of knowing her sisters were safe was more than enough to quell the remains of the little child Lizzie had once been.

~ ~ ~ ~ ~

It was a crisp cool Wednesday afternoon in February when Lizzie walked up the aisle of St Cuthbert's Church, holding old Tom's arm. Granny Eliza, flanked by Lizzie's sisters wiped the tears from her eyes. "Oh my! What an angel you are, Lizzie," admiring Lizzie's long sleeved cream coloured wedding dress, trimmed with blue ribbon and lace. As Lizzie stood there, she felt the babe in her belly, flutter.

Adam's mother smiled over at her. She was happy that Adam had chosen Lizzie for a bride. She had always had a soft spot for the girl knowing how hard she had worked alongside Granny Eliza. A girl like Lizzie would always take care of her own.

Reaching the alter steps, Lizzie felt a sense of happiness she could hardly contain and she glanced at the handsome man that in a few minutes would be her husband.

The vicar bowed his head. "We are gathered here today to join this man and woman in holy matrimony..."

It seemed minutes had barely past before Lizzie heard the bells ringing out joyously and she was on the arm of her husband as he led her lovingly out into the cold crisp air.

Epilogue

December 1882

Snow had started falling heavily by the second week of December. Granny Eliza had been shopping for her Christmas baking. "Oh she's a marvel, our little Rose, just like her mother." she declared to anyone who would listen. "For one that came so early, she is as tough as a babe as I ever did see." If Granny Eliza thought other than this, she never let on, but she made certain no one else would dare to suggest anything else.

Adam had come home with a surprise Christmas tree. When Lizzie and her sisters saw it, they gaped open mouthed as Adam lugged it through the house to the parlour. Lizzie and Adam, Martha and Annie decorated it with candles and tinsel, and their lovingly created handmade ornaments. On Christmas day there would be juicy oranges, nuts and gifts to claim from the branches.

On December 23rd Adam had brought home the goose from the butcher that Granny Eliza specified he order it from, and presented it to Lizzie. "It's the fattest goose he ever had," Adam said, referring to the butcher, "and he said to let you know that he had it saved, especially for you! What do you think he meant by that?" Lizzie laughed. "Only that I didn't want a scrawny one." Adam shook his head at her and kissed her forehead.

On Christmas Eve, large flakes of snow drifted down from the heavens as the family walked the distance to St Cuthberts for the late service. Tomorrow would be Christmas. The luscious aroma of roasted root vegetables, sage and onion stuffed goose, and plum pudding would fill the house. Adam's mother would arrive, bringing gifts for everyone, and cradling little Rose in her arms. She would say "If only my own dear mother were alive to meet this dear child, but I know she is looking down from above." Adam would give his mother a hug, knowing how very much her family meant to her. Granny Eliza and Tom would arrive, and Granny Eliza would bring her special mince pies. It occurred to Lizzie, as she entered the old, sacred church, that her wishes for Christmas had somehow, miraculously, come true.

The End.

Printed in Great Britain
by Amazon